Boroughs of the Dead

Short Stories

Andrea Janes

Five of these stories were previously published under the name A.J. Sweeney. *A Fitting Tribute* first appeared in Lightning Flash e-zine in May, 2011. *Nethermead* first appeared in Flashes in the Dark e-zine in January, 2011. *Morbus* first appeared in Golden Visions Magazine in August, 2011. *Newtown Creek* first appeared in The Horror Zine in October, 2011. *We'll All Be in the Arms of our True Loves Before Long* appeared in Bards & Sages Quarterly in October, 2011.

CONTENTS

ACKNOWLEDGMENTS

This book is dedicated to my friends and family, who helped me, supported me, and let me blather on about ghosts for two years while never once letting their eyes glaze over. Most of all, I dedicate this to my husband Robert Sweeney.

WE'LL ALL BE IN THE ARMS OF OUR TRUE LOVES BEFORE LONG

I reproduce here without alteration the diary of Dr. Charles H_____ in order to defend the strange actions that have lately brought his reputation under scrutiny. As a man of science, I believe it will testify to his utter innocence of any wrongdoing by virtue of what seems to be, in my medical opinion, an acute nervous condition.

Signed, Dr. Nathaniel W_____, M.D.

Diary of Dr. Charles H_____, M.D.

December 22nd, 1799

I blame the episode on lack of sleep and on the blizzard.

Long past midnight, the savage unrelenting wind moaned outside my window, and I tossed and turned, shunned by slumber. Illuminated by the driving white snow, my bedroom seemed unnaturally bright, like the eyes of a fever patient.

I was lying in bed, wide-awake and staring, when I suddenly heard a singularly hideous shriek. I strained my ears and tried to make out from whence it came; it was impossible to tell with the noise of the wind, but I looked instinctively in the direction of the window.

I saw nothing there but swirling whiteness.

When I turned my eyes again to the interior of my room, I found myself confronted with the apparition of a young woman standing not two inches away from me. Her mouth opened and closed soundlessly as if forming inaudible words or gasping for air. I stood still and watched her, not knowing what to do, and before I could comprehend the situation or do anything sensible, she disappeared.

The hallucination had more of an effect on me than I realized.

Nathaniel said I was behaving strangely this morning. We were walking through the snowdrifts to our clinic, and I apparently gazed at Lispenard's marsh for quite some time. Boys were clearing snow from it to make a skating rink, and I am told I watched them as if in a trance, staring into the gray, befogged surface of the frozen water. I cannot say why I did this, or for how long, but when I came out of this state, I heard my colleague saying, "They're only clearing the ice."

Later, when darkness fell and our patients had gone, we went into the cellar for anatomization, as we often do. A nearby charity hospital supplies our cadavers and after office hours we open up the city's indigent dead in search of secrets to cure the living. Lately, we have been testing new theories delineating the vascular system, sifting through networks of ropy veins like explorers cataloguing a system of rivers on a map. My colleague and I are determined to be at the forefront of scientific thought, and I normally see nothing gruesome in what is a commonplace practice among our brotherhood of physicians.

This night, unfortunately, our cadaver was female, and I caught myself staring pensively at her pallid face. I moved my hands over the body with a strange tenderness, thinking the whole time of the apparition, and found myself trembling as I made an incision in the right forearm.

"What is wrong with you?" Nathaniel demanded. "You are somewhere else tonight!"

3

Foolishly, I told him of the apparition. "Well, it isn't her, of course" he said, divining my irrational thoughts. "The woman you saw last night was only a trick of the light or perhaps a somnambulist vision." It is imperative that anatomization be conducted with a minimum of morbidity and superstition, and he was distinctly irritated by my foolish behavior. He called an early end to our session.

We walked home in silence past merry bands of ice skaters, our mutual glumness contrasting with their gay shouts that rang out clear as bells in the silver night. We passed the half-empty wooden carts of the water-works, their labor temporarily halted by the snow and ice. The water-works have lately been buying up territory in the neighborhood; their hammers and pickaxes are the chief source of daytime noise as they dig into the underground springs that crisscross beneath the town. Now all was quiet as drifts of snow piled up atop the new well and the subterranean streams beneath us were frozen and still.

December 24th, 1799

A copy of the *Gazette* lies on the desk before me. I have been staring at it all morning.

"This is she," I'd said, when the paper arrived. A sketch of her, an exact likeness, graced the front page along with the headline 'Young girl missing!'

"So this is your 'apparition.'" My colleague examined the broadsheet. "I know her. She lives in the boarding house next to mine. The neighbors say she eloped."

"No," said I. "She is dead."

Now Nathaniel is studiously ignoring me. I am supposed to be writing up notes on a gouty patient, but I cannot focus. Last night was another wakeful one; I was troubled again by strange noises: echoes and vibrations and a hollow knocking sound, such as I have heard when the men from the water company sound the wooden pipes to test the depths of their well. It calls to mind loose cargo knocking around in a ship's hull. I do not tell my colleague, for he will only say that I'm hallucinating. Bah! I am not hallucinating!

December 26th, 1799

Again I fail to sleep. A cold air permeates my bedroom, and I cannot get warm. I am wrapped under blankets, a fire is in the grate, and my maid has left me a hot water bottle; still a chill creeps over my skin and will not leave me. This has been a miserable Christmas; I am sick at home and ill with fever for two days now.

December 27th, 1799

I can hear a woman screaming, though there is no blizzard tonight. It is audible, and yet it seems that no one can hear it except me. She is calling to me; I am sure of it. I look for her, but I cannot see her. From my window, I can see a tremendous sunset over Lispenard's meadow, whose expanse stretches all the way to the wide, frozen river. It is a gorgeous, unholy blood-red sunset that is gaspingly beautiful yet provokes some discomfort in me, for it lights the fields of snow up in red until they resemble a sea of blood. I am forced to take another tincture of opium to calm my nerves.

December 28th, 1799

We have found each other.

Tonight Nathaniel and I closed up the office early for the holiday. He invited me to spend New Year's Eve with him at Trinity Church, to take in mass and the ringing of the bells with him and his wife. I declined, citing lingering fever, and told him I would see him when the office opened again in January. I felt the need to be alone.

As I walked home, I became engrossed in my thoughts and rather lost track of time.

Before long the sun had fallen, and I found myself alone on the slushy streets, chill and wet with melting snow. I realized I'd been walking in circles.

Suddenly I felt a faint pressure on the small of my back, and I shivered in the cool air. A voice, very close to my ear, said faintly: "Please." The spirit, for that is the only word I can think to call it, led me down the dusky evening streets. When it stopped, I was standing in front of the new well.

It whispered again, "Please."

I walked toward the well.

I leaned over and pushed aside the wet, heavy snow. There I saw it: her white face in the well's dreadful depths, one hand pressed against the icy surface. She was even more beautiful in flesh than she had been as a wraith.

I know what to do.

December 29th, 1799

I rose late this morning, still recovering from last night. Very late last evening I sent my most discreet servant out to fetch me vast quantities of ice; he did so without questions or hesitation, just as he'd prepared her chamber.

Once the ice had been procured – he cut it out of Lispenard's meadow – I went back to the well. It was nearly three o'clock in the morning, and no one saw me take the water-works' pickaxe and cut into the surface of the frozen well. No one saw me lift out her rigid body.

Revivification following death has eluded physicians for centuries; I posit, however, that when preserved by extreme cold, all the human systems and faculties remain viable and can be reanimated if properly treated. She is still packed in ice. The warming of the body must be done very delicately, and before I cut, I must plan. Measure twice, cut once, as they say.

December 31st, 1799

I am frustrated. I have been up since last night trying to adequately warm the body.

It was easy to tell from the bruises that she had been strangled. Gently I cut into her throat and replaced her trachea with a rubber tube. It is a beautiful throat, soft and slender. My eyes filled with tears of hate for the brute who killed her. I sewed the tube in gently. It will serve her well when she commences breathing again.

A machine of compressed air to force warm drafts into the lungs would have sufficed to begin the warming process, but only on a living body. Camphor, taken orally, is another solution, but again, can only re-warm a living body, as these systems must be functioning, however slightly, in order for these remedies to take effect. The warming of a corpse begins with cavity lavage.

I had to transport her to the anatomization room, for I lacked the proper equipment at home. I transported her as I would a living body suffering from extreme cold, in blankets, wrapped up warm and dry.

There was already a cadaver on the table, which I pushed aside. I lay the girl down gently and kissed her throat over the suture.

More tubing was required for the cavity lavage, as well as a solution of warm salt-water. This was a difficult process, for it was nearly impossible to remain impassive while inserting the tubing into her and I admit I was pale and shaken by the end of it. But it must be done, and it was done. Her stomach and bladder began to swell up, and a slight warmth did indeed begin to radiate from her.

Next, I attempted to circulate an intravenous injection of hot blood through the body. I used sheep's blood for this. Here I ran into difficulties. Her own blood was completely clogged in her veins; dried out, it refused to flow. The sheep's blood merely spurted back at me, or seeped and dribbled out onto the table and floor.

I pondered this difficulty as I massaged her arms, legs and heart. It has now become apparent that I have failed with the sheep's blood and will have to use my own.

Knowing the state of her veins, I decided to change the injection site. I am transfusing my blood directly into the vena cava at fifteen-minute intervals.

My sense of urgency increases; I have had the anatomization room to myself for nearly twenty-four hours but my colleague will be down come Monday morning. I will, therefore, increase the quantity, frequency and duration of the transfusion until I restore her to life and beauty again…

* * *

The diary ends here. On the morning of January 2nd, 1800, I found the small notebook next to Charles's body on the floor of the anatomization room. The room looked like the scene of a crime. It was readied with a number of instruments unfamiliar to me. Charles lay slumped over the corpse of the missing girl. Their arms were entangled grotesquely.

I felt both bodies for a pulse, but she was obviously long deceased, and he had clearly suffered extreme blood-loss.

A third cadaver lay amid the vast quantities of blood that coated the floor, half congealed. I identified it as one of our test subjects.

Most appalling of all: the girl's heart, attached to Charles by means of a rubber tube, had been pumped full of blood to the point of bursting. The exploded muscle lay in scattered shreds around the table. Blood was still leaking futilely from Charles' arm.

I cannot explain why, based on the work we conducted together, Dr. H____ imagined he would be able to perform this grossly unscientific necromancy unless he was in an addled state of mind induced by the fever of which he writes in his diary. I suspect his solitude also weighed heavy on him. Furthermore, I noted the absence of about half our supply of opium, none of which can be accounted for by our patients, a supply of such quantity as to induce hallucinations and madness in any individual taking that amount (about 7 grains per 12 hours).

Two days following his death, I went to Charles's house to dismiss his servants and pay off their wages. His is a much larger dwelling than I realized, and there are quarters in it I didn't know existed. My friend was wealthier than I imagined. I do not envy him, of course; I would rather have my modest income and sensible wife than all the money he possessed. Look at what happiness it brought him!

As I paid off the servants, one of them asked me what I was going to do with "the chamber." I did not know of what he spoke, so he led me to the attic. There I saw a woman's bedroom, all readied for a new bride, with a diamond ring on the pillow.

This story was inspired by the real-life murder of Elma Sands in 1799. She was killed by her fiancé, Levi Weeks, and stuffed in a well at the corner of Spring and Greene Streets in what is today known as SoHo. Levi Weeks was acquitted by a dream-team of defense attorneys, and Elma Sands' cousin cursed them when the verdict was read: "If ye die a natural death I shall believe there is no God in Heaven!" Those attorneys were Alexander Hamilton and Aaron Burr.

A FITTING TRIBUTE

By the time she came to live with us, Aunt Anne was already dying.

I watched as her dark carriage rode up to the house, slick and wet in the rain. Papa was anxious and told the servants to draw her a hot bath immediately. I know he fretted because her illness reminded him of my poor consumptive mother. But she was not my mother and this was not her house. She was an interloper intruding on the kingdom I had built with Papa in our city by the sea. I was just a little girl when we sailed here from France. "This all belongs to you now," Papa told me that day when our ship cut through the glittering harbor. The shining rivers were mine, the tall brick buildings were mine, the shimmering church spires towering above everything were mine, too, but most of all, our house was mine.

And now this intruder had come.

I sat in my dressing room the night she arrived, brushing my hair and listening to her. She'd been given the set of rooms next to mine – a large bedroom, a sitting room, and a bath. The dressing room adjoined our suites in the middle. I could hear her, could hear the water splash as she got out of the tub, hear her walk toward the dressing room.

She seemed startled to see me sitting there. "Didn't you expect to be sharing your suite?" I asked coolly, staring at her in the large mirror as I worked the brush through my hair.

I held the hand mirror at an angle to see the back of my head. My hair was thick and black and glossy, curling into lush, deep waves. She watched me scrutinize myself in the vertex of the two mirrors and said, "What a vain child you are."

"I think it would be vainer still to have a maid do my coiffure. To be fussed over."

"And now instead of a maid you have an old aunt." She took my silver brush and began to work it through my hair slowly but without gentleness. "How lucky you are to have such fine hair," she said, fixing her gaze on me.

Her eyes were large and wide-set, almost bulbous, pale green-gray and watery. The ridge of her nose was curved and sharp, her skin waxy. She had a face like a Hapsburg with that weak, turtle-like chin, crooked teeth and string-bean mouth. How she could be related to me by blood I did not understand.

She caught me looking at her just as my eyes were roving over the great expanse of her forehead. Armies could do battle on that forehead; there was room enough. Perhaps I giggled or smirked because suddenly she looked very cross.

"You know, you won't be sixteen forever," she said, glaring at me, "When you become my age, you will awake one day to find your beauty gone. It will never return."

And with that she pulled off her wig.

At dinner that night I hardly said anything. Anne spoke of all her friends back in Paris, the Chatillons and who-knows-else, and Papa listened ardently. I sat there trying to banish from my mind the image of those dry patches of colorless hair clinging to her lumpy, denuded skull and trying not to laugh.

After dinner, as she and Papa sat downstairs by the fire drinking brandy, I crept into her room. My, but she had a lot of clothing! Dozens of dresses, forests of furs, and hats, of course – hundreds. But what really amused me were the wigs. She had them on funny little heads, combed out or piled high in various styles, all the same shade of brown – as if she was fooling anyone!

The next day I paid a visit to the shop where I often bought costumes for my dance recitals. They were specialists in period dress and accessories, and I found just the thing for dear, dear Aunt Anne.

I could hardly wait until four o'clock when the delivery would come. I tried to read but kept jumping up and looking out the window. Aunt Anne glanced at me from where she was stationed by the fire under her fur blanket – that ridiculous fur blanket! – no doubt to evoke Papa's sympathies to greater effect, and snapped, "What are you so excited about?"

The bell rang, and moments later a servant appeared with a large box. "For you madame." She placed it in Aunt Anne's lap.

"Oh, a gift!" I exclaimed. "Have you got a young admirer?"

She glared at me and opened the box – pulling out an enormous white-powdered wig in the style of Louis XIV.

I laughed so hard, I was on the ground in tears.

Now, Aunt Anne also liked to play the flute. This was her great passion. (At least something was touching those lips of hers!) When she played on warm afternoons, my girlfriends and I would often dance under her window, howling up at her, "Oh play, play! Charm us with your ancient pagan sounds, O goddess of love!" This brought us great amusement, though one day Papa caught us and punished me.

"How dare you mock a sick woman!" he thundered. He sent my friends home and sent me to my room where I sat and laughed to myself, playing the episode over in my mind. What fun a girl could have with a humorless spinster aunt!

That evening she struck back – in her own unimaginative way. I went into my powder room to find my favorite bottle of perfume missing. It was a delicate, orange-scented concoction they called Florida-water in those days, and I wore it always. I suppose she thought the game was on, but I ignored her. The next night my combs and hand-mirror were gone, and the third sunset found the bristles of my hairbrush burned to ash. Next, she had the servants remove the mirror over my dressing table.

Now, I felt that she was becoming less amusing and more of an irritant. I grew tired of playing with my little mouse of an auntie and decided it was time she go.

I made up my mind how to do it. I had no small talent for drawing, and I applied myself industriously to this endeavor most evenings. I began to spend several hours at a time in my study, working away quietly, sketching and drafting, designing a lovely and fitting tribute to my beloved aunt.

There was alchemy in my work. With every line I drew, I dreamed of the day she would die, willing her demise into being. With each mark of the pencil, my energy transmuted the lead into a magic spell I wove around us both. This was not the first time I had effected the demise of a competitor. For you see, I was born with a special gift. I don't know how, and I don't know why, but very early on in my life, I noticed something about myself: whatever I wanted, I got. For instance, if I made up my mind that I would get, say, an apple, within hours there would be a fruit peddler at the door. If I wanted to dance the lead in *Giselle*, I had simply to think it. If another girl was bothering me in school, it wasn't unlikely that she would soon become very sick and be forced to spend the rest of the term in the country.

As I grew older, I became more artful. It wasn't just about wanting things and getting them. It was, rather, a game I played with the universe. This particular game, I decided, was going to be won with grace and style. What's more, this one would create an eternal monument to my art.

The night my drawing was finished, I dressed slowly, leisurely, and wore my hair loose, streaming down in dark waves. I pinned the forelocks back with garnet and amethyst combs, admiring the way they brought out my eyes. The face is the picture, they say, and the hair is the frame.

"Why, my dear," Papa said, "Don't you look lovely." All evening I smiled and chatted and laughed gaily, and Anne sat pale and silent in her seat.

"Aunt Anne has been so quiet tonight," I said after dinner. "Perhaps you'd like to open a gift I made for you. Won't that cheer you up, dear Auntie?"

She opened it, and the room fell silent. There, framed and mounted, was a drawing of her tomb, a monument with the swirling Gothic towers so in fashion right now, with curlicues abounding. Two slender spires flanked an arched canopy within which was a carved bas-relief reading simply "de Cresserons," our surname.

"I've designed it for you, dear Auntie," I said, putting my slim, white arm around her. "As a measure of my devotion."

"You are too kind," she replied, her face ashen. "Excuse me," she said weakly, "I must go to bed."

I smiled at her retreating form and thought, "I win."

Within the week she was dead.

For a while, I felt deliciously unburdened. My world was as it should be, and my home was my own again.

Then one night, about a fortnight after she died, I was just getting into bed when something strange happened. As I pulled the covers up to my chin – for it was a very cold night – something made me gasp. I don't know what it was, nor can I recall exactly the order in which things took place, but the end result of it was that I seemed to have breathed in rather too sharply through my mouth. Somehow I felt a strange tickle as though a bit of hair or dust were lodged in my throat. Just stuck there, tickling me, making me cough. That in and of itself might not have given me pause, but there was something familiar in the air that did. I smelled the sweet smell of Florida-water and I knew she had not gone.

There were other signs that she was still around.

Not once could I leave my room without returning to find everything in disarray, books and papers strewn all about. My clothing was found scissored into slivers. One morning all of my perfume bottles were smashed at once right in front of me; one of the shards cut me.

One night, as I lay in bed unsleeping, I heard the most indescribable noise pervading my room. Try as I might, I could not guess what it was; I only knew that it was Anne, and she was playing another game with me. The best I can say is that it sounded like a shuffling noise, like cloth being brushed and folded perhaps, or, more accurately, dragged across the floor. Curiosity triumphed over fear, and I lit my candle.

Her wigs, every one of them, moved across the floor of their own accord. They seemed to dance, so light were their movements, like leaves in the wind. All across my floor they drifted, tangled tumbleweeds of hair executing delicate fouettés. All of a sudden I felt something brush up against my neck – it was the powdered wig, the Louis XIV wig, moving itself against me for all the world like a kitten who wants to be stroked.

There were occurrences in the daytime as well. Clocks would strike at all hours, never corresponding to the time. Once I heard it strike thirty-seven times before the maid snatched it off the wall with a look of terror. "Why did you stop it?" I asked, "I wanted to see how far it could go." She looked at me. "Bah! You're becoming strange." Was I? Perhaps a change was coming over me. I began to wonder if others could see it, if they could tell that I was haunted.

Another night I awoke to hear the sound of footsteps in my room. It was she. I heard her slip across the room in the darkness and come very near to me, thinking I was asleep. I was shocked to hear the sharp silver sound of scissors snipping right next to my ear! My hand flew up to my hair — ragged chunks were missing. The servants and I looked, but we never found any on the floor or blankets or anywhere else.

Soon the servants had stopped coming into our — my — wing of the house at all.

"You wait," I told her. "Soon I shall be rid of you."

For the tomb that I had drawn had finally been built, and I knew that once we — joy of joys! — put my aunt in the stone walls I designed for her and consecrated her tomb, her spirit would leave our house for good.

The eve of her burial arrived at last. I dressed as though for a party, adorning myself with every bauble Papa ever gave me. I gazed at myself in the dressing room mirror: my eyes were bright, and my amethyst combs shone amid glossy curls. I had to arrange them more artfully this time, to hide the locks of hair that were missing. As I dressed, I smelled the Florida-water and saw a white hand in the mirror's reflection, rested gently on my shoulder. Just a hand, nothing more. I slapped it and said, "Tomorrow we bury you," and it disappeared.

I made my way downstairs. Outside was a howling night of snow and hail, but inside was warm and merry, filled with the smells of roast duck and pink bunches of hothouse roses, my favorite flower. I sat down to dinner under Papa's admiring gaze and began to eat daintily.

Without warning, I began to cough. "Excuse me," I said, but I couldn't stop. There was that tickle in my throat again. There was definitely something caught – I coughed again, more violently. Papa stared at me, but I no longer had any choice in the matter. Perhaps not as subtly as I'd have liked, I reached into my mouth and pulled out a long, black, shining hair. My own. He gasped. I looked down at my plate. Gone was the roast duck and, in its place, masses of damp, dark, curling black tresses. The hair lay there like a newborn creature, dark and slick and glistening, covered in slime.

I coughed again and pulled another hair from my mouth, and then another. More and more, not single strands now, but huge hunks that I hacked out nauseatingly. They fell on my plate in wet clumps as I clawed them out of my throat. My body spasmed and I vomited wet, black hair.

Mortified, I ran from the table.

I collapsed in the hall, falling to my knees in a fresh fit of coughing, tearing at my throat as my body spasmed again. "She cannot breathe!" Papa cried out. The servants gathered around and tried to aid me, but there was seemingly no end to the obstruction in my throat…

She is here again, wafting the sweet scent of Florida-water, pressing her hands against my throat. I cannot slap them away this time. I am too weak; I cannot breathe. I hear her whisper, very close to my ear, "I win."

As darkness descends, I have a vision of a tomb that says "de Cresserons." My last thought before I die is that I will have to share it with her.

A FISH STORY

Dedicated to Herman Melville

The night we met I was meandering through the watery alleys of Lower Manhattan, so absorbed in my own thoughts that had you not called out my name I would not have stopped at all as I passed you.

Admittedly, your outward aspect singularly perturbed me, as you were so extremely familiar of face, and still so strange. Yet when you bade me stroll with you a while I acquiesced, for what else could I do?

I suppose we made a cosy enough pair, you and I, as we strolled through the lamplight. We were exactly alike in height and gait; from a distance one would have supposed we were twins. We walked in silence until I asked you "Shall we go north or south?" when we rounded the corner at Pearl Street.

"Oh, south," you murmured. "Wall Street is as desolate as a ghost town at night, don't you find?"

Of course I agreed.

Finally I could not help but ask you, "What is it you want?"

"I want? I seek you not. It is you that seekest me."

"I?"

"I know what you were thinking as you walked the streets tonight. You were thinking about our work."

Yes, I had been.

"You were thinking how trifling it is."

It was true. I had been.

"A monumental work must be written," you said to me. "We both know it must. There can be no more of these sailor's romances. A truer tale awaits us, a tale that must be told. A tale that speaks of your true self."

I heard myself say: "I seek but cannot find this monumental tale. I feel I'll have to dash my very brains against the rocks and pull the story out of the all blood and wreckage." My words poured forth as though you had cast a veritable spell on me. "There are unknowable truths but I know I can hunt them down."

"Fame is fair game to anybody who can catch it."

Fame! I should have known then, as I spoke of truth and you of fame that we would never reconcile the two.

As we stood there in the darkening alleys, I saw my future suddenly swim before me; its shadows and vague outlines were mere skeletons, but there was a story sketched upon them.

You were the tell-tale, pointing me toward the water and the direction in which I knew I had to go. You beckoned me to the end of Coenties Slip. I followed you down, and soon we were at the edge of the water.

Your face was the last thing I saw before I submerged.

I plunged down into the blackness and saw in those depths a tide of words, a sea of ideas, an unfathomable loneliness.

The current wanted to take me out to where the sea and rivers mingled. If it wants me, I thought, let it have me. I was swept away and the words that I saw swimming there were far too grand not to chase. Out in the depths I was alone. All the eerie, gleaming creatures of the deep were far away and there was nothing but empty silence. The water was murky; I could not see. The waves were lapping at my throat. The loneliness was ungodly and the current was very cold.

I began to feel I was no longer in the ocean. For a moment my eyes stung too much to open, but presently I managed to squeeze my lids apart. When I did, it became apparent to me that I was in an enormous cavern filled with dull and sullen reddish light. I felt as though I were waking from a deep sleep. As my eyes brought the darkness into focus, I realized this stagnant abyss was no cavern – I was deep inside a veritable maze of bones. Between the bones were soft tissues of flesh and, at my feet, a shallow pool of fetid water with some tiny fish still jumping and swimming in it. "It can't be…" I whispered. "I must be dreaming."

A small, rough axe materialized in my hand and suddenly, uncannily, dreadfully, I knew that whatever had brought me here ordained I should have to cut my way out. And so I hacked at the insides of the poor beast's belly. "I am sorry to have to cut through your guts so rudely," I thought as I tore into him, "but you know I can't stay in here."

Cutting through him was a massive undertaking and, no matter how industriously I worked, there always seemed to be more and more of him. The flesh, I found, wasn't flesh at all but that strange substance known as blubber. It was gelatinous and very pale, and its soft, unresisting texture made it difficult to cut. If I tried to hack into it like one would a rock in a cavern or tangled vines deep in a jungle, prodigious oozings of new fat would appear immediately to take its place, though I could discern not from whence they came. I was becoming frustrated until I realized it could be pulled in strips. Once I figured that out I merely grabbed a good solid end of it and ripped it upward, forming a sort of doorway.

Unsure of what lay beyond it, I moved with caution but soon discovered it was just a matter of cutting my way through a bit more skin – a wall, really, but only three inches thick (such a delicate covering for the epidermis of this massive creature!) Because I had carefully made my blubber-door between two of the great, curving, shining ribs, the vaulted ceilings of which brought ecclesiastical thoughts to mind, all that barred me from freedom was this thin skin which soon was breached.

I was out to sea again.

What was this new adventure? A dream within a dream? It would seem so and yet I was beginning to have my doubts about the oneiric nature of this journey. The water felt too cold and deep, produced a chill in me too real to have come from the realm of sleep. Where will you take me next, I wondered. Where will your seething breakers take me, where next will your furious lashings fling me?

To my surprise I wasn't pulled farther out to sea but merely floated up to the surface of the water where I was borne upon a wave. What message was this? What was I to do now? Perhaps a truer poet than I would have thrown himself farther into the ocean but I fear the sober Dutch blood in my veins prevailed. I did the commonplace thing: I swam toward home.

I went easily through the Narrows, for swimming in saltwater is as riding in a spring-carriage to a practiced swimmer, but as I came in through the bay I met with a staggering sight.

There, floating upon the surface of the calm waters were dozens, literally dozens, of whale carcasses.

There wasn't any other way to do it: if I wanted to get home I would have to swim through them.

There is no name for the feeling this realization produced in me. All around was horror and blood and an appalling hell of decay. The waves were pointed triangles of water lapping like little teeth against the dead fish awash with streaks of bloody foam like the effluvia of a rabid animal. The whales themselves looked as though they had been sucked into and spit out by a maelstrom; I could imagine them flying through the sky into a collision of waves.

There are no words for the sensation swimming by the animals produced in me, however vividly I can recall it. It filled me with dread to slide between their corpses, my hands and arms brushing against the gleaming, ghastly bodies of the great fishes, their masses of flesh all covered in sticky slime. Each stroke evoked the indescribable sensation of moving through the deepest death.

The bloody water was tinctured as though with young claret. It is most disconcerting to see water that violent color – it isn't meant to be, for water is supposed to soothe the human spirit with its lulling shades of blues and greens. To see it so was to witness an inversion of nature itself. Everywhere it was the brightest vermillion and its brightness contrasted hideously with the dull-grey of whale-skin.

The animals themselves lay so helpless and prostrate on their backs, their bellies pointed helplessly upward to heaven all heaped together, that sometimes there was only the slimmest channel to swim through between two of their bodies. Some of them lay on their sides so that their narrow lower jaws jutted out like useless flaps into the water. To see their grandeur thus reduced shattered my spirit and I, I suppose to save myself from going mad, let myself slip into a kind of trance. I thought not about the vileness of the scene in which I found myself but rather let my thoughts launch themselves into the ether, far above where I, so far from shore, so utterly deserted by my fellow man, swam alone through the bloody harbor of dead whales. These thoughts attached themselves to visions of life itself and death, and what it means to be a solitary man alone upon the sea.

By the time I got to shore, I had the idea for my book.

Sodden and quivering did I arrive upon the soggy shores of Manhattan Island. I staggered to my home, and my wife gasped when she saw me at the door.

"I know," I said, holding out my hand to her, "what I must look like – "

She screamed and ran from me, ran right upstairs to where you sat at our writing desk.

"Oh Mister Melville," she said to you, wringing her hands together.

"What is it, Beth?" you asked.

"I saw something just now on the stairs – it looked like, Oh! the very image of you – but drowned! Oh, dead you were, and drowned!"

And you petted her head and reassured her there were no such things as ghosts, and we watched her as she walked away.

We wrote the book together, you and I, the book that only an author from the dead could have written. Which of us was dead? I know not. I go. You go. He goes. Ye go. Some mysteries are too vast for men to comprehend, and to answer these riddles is to dive deeper than Melville can go.

NETHERMEAD

She couldn't put her finger on it but something felt wrong.

She'd been walking for what seemed like hours, though she couldn't tell for sure. She looked at her phone. The battery was dead. She had no watch.

It was a cool, misty evening in late winter, almost spring, and it had still been light out when she got home from work. It had seemed a shame to shut herself inside and watch TV, so she put on her boots and walked to the park.

She wandered through the muddy meadows and naked trees, feeling herself relax almost immediately, slipping into a meditative state as she rounded the still, gray pond. If there was one thing she was good at, it was emptying her mind. She once took a yoga class and sat there in guilty silence when the instructor lamented how difficult it was to get your mind really empty. She didn't dare mention this happened to her without effort nearly all the time.

She worked as a dispatcher for a shipping company, which meant she assigned one thing from one person to be moved from one place to another place by another person. After five years of dull routine, she began to feel a generalized lull taking hold of her mind.

It wasn't unpleasant. It allowed her to field calls from angry customers with robotic detachment, and go through the motions on her long, routine-filled weekends that mainly consisted of the supermarket, Laundromat, and solitary movies. No, truly there was nothing wrong with the mellow emptiness she allowed herself to feel, but things became problematic when the mellowness gave way to carelessness and forgetfulness.

She often felt a vague, foggy feeling that she was forgetting something but she couldn't remember what it was. This feeling nagged her now as she plodded through the park. "Am I late to meet someone? Not likely. More likely I'm forgetting something...."

She continued on her way, letting the susurrus of water relax her as she walked nearer to the bridge and brook. As the pleasant murmuring sound grow louder in the distance she realized it was the ravings of a homeless man who trod back and forth on the bridge. "Beyond the infrastructure, beyond the sales tax. A hundred million jobs, that's all we got," he said. He stared at the sky. "Before 1991, before Columbus, tribal era, medicine man…" She changed course without breaking stride. "I'll go over by the hill instead," she said to herself.

There were a number of steep hills in the park, and now she rounded the base of the tallest of these, Lookout Hill, which ended its western vista quite abruptly over a stony cataract of loose shale and jagged boulders. The meadow beyond was called Nethermead. Past this she strolled, letting the sound of birdsong drown out the vagrant as he shouted about Helen Keller and electrical wire.

The night was getting dark and damp; the lamplights would be coming on soon. Her eyes were having trouble discerning the dusky shapes coming at her in the distance. Four loose-limbed youths, all male, were on the path coming toward her. She felt herself stiffen slightly and held her breath a little as they got nearer.

One of them said, "The hours are a good – "

His friend interrupted. "Better than the ER?"

"Way better. The hours at the ER were brutal."

And she realized these four young men were doctors, or perhaps medical students. She laughed a little and felt herself relax again.

The park had become very still and quiet. The evening had turned pleasantly misty, enveloping her in a soothing blankness. A strange, not-unpleasant fatigue, a blissful sensation, washed warmly over her; she felt as though she were almost falling asleep, as though she could lie down and take a nap right there on the ground.

Her mind was so befogged, she was unaware of a lone man walking about twelve feet behind her. He caught up to her quickly with his long strides and she started a little as he walked beside her, matching his pace to hers. "Are you going home now?" he asked in awkward, accented English. He was smiling. "Yes, I'm going home now," she answered. He smiled again and nodded. "Okay." And he walked away in the direction from which he'd come.

She began to feel that old, vague, uneasy sense that there was something she was supposed to do, but she couldn't remember what it was.

"Have I forgotten something? Am I late to meet someone? Not likely. More likely I'm forgetting something…."

The evening mist, so charming moments ago, now seemed impenetrable. Twilight caused solid shapes to shift. She walked down one path only to realize she was going in the opposite direction she'd intended. She turned around to find she'd come round the bend and ended up where she started.

"I've been here before…"

She wondered absently if she was losing her mind. She had been making more mistakes at work than usual, pressing the wrong button here, entering the wrong data code there.

A dreadful shiver ran through her. Though it was definitely dark, the lamplights hadn't come on. Another oddity: she hadn't seen another soul since the strange man in the woods. But oddest of all was the birdsong: it had disappeared completely. All was completely and utterly silent and still.

Steadily she walked, slowly yielding to the sense of inevitability that was spreading over her. And then at last, she saw a landmark, something distinct from the seemingly endless spiral of pathways and trees: Lookout Hill.

Automatically, she walked toward it and up the zig-zagging paths that circumscribed its steep sides. Back and forth until she reached the top. The fog and mist were such that it took her a moment to register what she saw when she looked down. It was *she*, walking on the path below. She mused for a moment, gazing down at herself.

Without thinking, she picked up a large rock with both hands and threw it down on her head. Her body below crumpled.

Now her mind felt clear, alert. As she stared at her own body lying below the hillside, she felt more lucid than she had in ages.

"That's better," she said.

THE *GENERAL SLOCUM*

It happened in June, the fifteenth of June. The promise of summer hung in the air. All was hot and clear and white and blue; what can go wrong in the beautiful, blissful month of June?

There was to be a church picnic that day. It was a Saturday -- *Samestag,* Saturn's day, Saturn who devoured his son. At the end of every Saturnalia, all debts must be paid. Didn't we pay our dues enough? We always worked hard. We prayed every day.

We were at work, all of us fathers. We did not go. Only our very hearts and souls went, the women, the children, our wives and our lives. We trusted Van Schaick and his crew.

The picnic was to be at Locust Point. Our wives packed sandwiches and sauerkraut. Our children brought their toys: kites and baseballs, hoops and sticks. We fathers were at work by eight; only Reverend Haas was there to see them off among the happy shouting, music and laughter!

My little Lili! My little Albert!

When we got home from work, we were greeted with newspaper headlines. They screamed at us the terrible news. Down the street, it is said that Emil Deurelein fainted when he heard. Six of them in his family, all lost.

Why did this happen to us?

* * *

Nobody ever thinks to ask me what I know. "She is nothing but an old lady," they say and laugh at me up their sleeves. I may be old and lame, a little deaf and somewhat blind, but I've seen more with my withered eyes than they ever have or ever will. I have had to make my own living, and it has toughened me. I took in sewing on Sunday afternoons. "She does not heed the doctrine of the church!" They say that about me, too. "She is not really one of us." Dour Lutherans though they be, I'd tell any one of them what I know if they'd only think to ask me. But they are too busy being pious. Being pious and suing Captain Van Schaiek.

From the park, I watched them strolling, laughing and singing; I followed, for I saw something among them that compelled me. I've always been able to see things before others saw them – I knew when I came home from market on that horrible Saturday forty-five years back that my husband was dead. I knew it before I even walked in the door. I always knew when it was going to rain, and I was always the first one out of the house in a fire. I could have been a faro sharper if I were a less honest woman. It's the second sight that got me through all these years alone. The devil himself couldn't hide from me.

Which is why I took notice on that very bonny day in June when the children and their mothers gathered in Tompkins Square Park. They saw nothing of the black pall that hung over them.

It was nothing but a shadow, without shape and without form. Black like a rain cloud, utterly invisible, I knew, to everyone but me. Reverend Haas caught my eye and smiled sanctimoniously. "Shall you be joining us today, Trudi?"

I haven't been to church since before his mummy stopped spanking his bare bottom. I merely met his smile with one of my own. "Should I tell him what I saw?" I wondered. I decided not to. Nobody likes an outspoken old lady, after all. And yet I was curious. "I shall walk with you all to the boat," I told him, noting his look of hastily concealed dismay.

I followed them as far as the pier.

The black cloud followed overhead along with them. I squinted, trying to see if I could make out a face. I heard some giggling; I know I must have looked quite the funny old woman grimacing up at the sky.

Not a single other person noticed it, nor did they see what I saw when we arrived at the pier on Third Street. The cloud began to shiver and shift. It sifted itself like dirty flour over the bodies and faces of the little children, but nobody noticed. From the dust, a shape began to gather and form. It swirled like a cyclone over the crowd and settled on the deck of the ship. It seemed to me to be vaguely human, but smaller – it was, I realized, an imp of sorts, an *alpern* type from whence come all our bad dreams. He pressed upon the crowd swarming up the gangplank; I felt him on my chest. I couldn't breathe. I could only watch, helpless, as they walked toward it. The little imp seemed to be dancing – how merry he seemed! But it was an evil dance, a *totentanz*, and I longed to tear my eyes from it and run away. Then he ceased dancing, stilled his clattering limbs and sniffed the air like a hound. He knew me. He knew I was there.

He looked at me. In the dusky indistinctness of his face, I saw his eyes like burning embers, and a grin that danced a jig with the corners of his mouth. Then he began to whistle. He whistled and danced, whistled and danced, and waved at me until I finally covered my face with my hands. He was waving, still, after the blast of the horn sounded and the children cheered and the ferryboat left for its last trip up the churning river.

* * *

Look at that old woman. She stares at me. She sees me!

Does she remember who I am? Or is she like the rest of them?

A long time ago, they used to write stories about me. They understood that I could walk among them, shift shape, disguise myself. Once upon a time we lived together. When women baked, they would leave me a little crumb here and there; now, everything has been swept clean. Once, they taught their children to tremble at my name; now when a child sees me he merely laughs – if he can see me at all! Once, their fathers crossed themselves when they shuttered the house at night; now, if I rattle through the corridors, they say it is the wind.

Did they lose their memories in the crossing? Is this where they forgot the old ways? They do not even know I'm here; they think they've replaced me with their new American god, he who lives among them, folded in their pockets. They have forgotten all that I have given them, all the stories I have told them, all the bargains they've struck with me. Their ancestors forgot our bargain once, a long time ago, and I drowned their children in the River Weser.

And now, after I have seen them safely to their new home, guaranteed their safe passage, watched out for their children in the heat waves and the darkness of this filthy new city, they forget me again. But I have not forgotten.

And so today I'll play my pipe again; we will all laugh and dance together. They will not even know I am among them, but soon, soon it will dawn on them whose music their children danced to.

Follow me, children, follow me! Tomorrow your papas will remember. They will remember that I have been here before. That I will be among my people until the rivers run red with the end of the world. Ignore me at your peril, for I can follow you everywhere. *Komme Kinder*, dance with me.

* * *

They were dead before they reached Hell Gate,

The lifeboats burned before the crew could lower them into the water. From their windows, the Blackwell's Island incurables watched the children and felt pity. Better to die of smallpox.

One thousand children dead and gone.

* * *

Wind sweeps the dust through our houses; echoes die in the empty streets. There is no more Little Germany. It may as well have been an earthquake, so utterly destroyed are our homes.

What will we fathers do now with no children to come home to?

Somewhere in the rubble of my broken heart, I find the shards of an old story. I try to put it back together but I can't remember how it goes. It was a rat-catcher who took the children, but I can't remember why. And why would he take them again?

What rat-catcher did we forget to pay?

For a thousand guilders, can we have them home again?

The General Slocum *was a ferryboat that crashed in June, 1904, with over 1,000 passengers, mainly women and children, aboard. Most belonged to a single German Lutheran parish in New York City's East Village. When the fathers of the community returned home from work that night, they learned that their wives and all their children had drowned.*

NEWTOWN CREEK

They said you could light the creek on fire.

That summer was the hottest I could remember but the heat didn't have anything to do with it, they said. It was because of the oil spill, and the mayor went on TV and said so and everything. But he didn't call it a spill; he called it a "leak."

I could hear the newscast from the other room as Jesse and I lay in our bunks playing Sailor. Sailor was a code name. We had lots of code names. Stealing candy bars from the corner deli was Packing A Wallop. Skipping out after lunch was a Double Feature. And Sailor was a game we played at night. The blue TV light flickered through the crack under the door and it all must have stayed with me as I fell asleep, because when I finally did I dreamed of water on fire.

In my dream it was the Upper Bay that was on fire, and the fire came from a raging battle. I watched from the Queensboro Bridge as the water turned red and burst into flame. Rusted ships screamed against each other with the clash of metal as they crashed, and guns and bombs rained fire. A lone man stood on the deck of one of the ships, commanding his armies to their deaths. He wore a tattered shirt and too-short bellbottoms; his face was covered with a ragged, brown beard. He looked at me over the expanse of the water and his eyes were wild and bloodshot. I woke up suddenly and sweat-soaked, and lay there listening to the whir of the fan on HIGH.

I was quiet at breakfast, watching condensation form on the carton of milk, the glasses of juice, our bowls of cereal. A drop of it dripped off the lip of the milk carton and landed on the tablecloth, turning its pale blue a dark, wet navy. The cereal box was damp and withered from the humidity.

"Let's go see the creek," Jesse said.

We walked over the train tracks and down 53rd Avenue, looking at the girls in their tube tops and short-shorts. We liked to play butt bingo, counting letters every time we saw a girl's ass hang out. Ass-cheek was a letter; so was cleavage, butt cleavage, and exposed midriffs. It seemed like every five seconds one of us was getting a boner and we'd have to stop and face the wall, laughing. I got ice from the deli and put it down my pants and we laughed our asses off because it looked like I peed myself. We showed my damp boner to Clive, the retarded kid down the street, and he started howling. We loved Clive, competing to make him laugh. It wasn't hard because Clive would laugh at an armpit fart.

The heat was bad enough as it was, but once you got within fifty feet of the canal, it was like walking directly behind the exhaust pipe of a city bus. It felt like I imagined the jungles would feel in Vietnam with all the Napalm and stuff, even though I'm not 100% sure what Napalm is. I was about to say that it would be cool to play War here but Jesse said, "We should bring some beers down here tonight." Said it like he did it all the time. Jesse's dream in life was to get girls to drink beer with us.

The water's edge was cordoned off but it was just police tape. We walked right under it -- there were no guards or anything.

The water was thick and brown, like paint. Jesse lit a match and threw it in. It really did burn. The flames were very low, small and blue, licking the top of the water. You could hardly tell it was on fire, except for the heat waves shimmering in the air. I kind of wished the flames would be huge, fifty-foot walls of fire. It wasn't the inferno I expected, but it was still awesome.

"This sucks," said Jesse, "Let's go."

We spent the rest of the day farting around the neighborhood, looking at girls. Damien Conners and his friends started playing Frisbee on Jackson Street and they chucked it at our heads until we left. Connors always picked on us because we were small and skinny and we had red hair. The ginger twins they called us. That was bullshit because our hair was starting to turn brown, and we are fourteen months apart.

We went home and I tried to work my dream into our comic book. Jesse did the drawings and I masterminded the story and all the dialogue. I decided the sailor was going to be a Greek named Kristos Bustos, but he was really Satan in disguise. Jesse wanted to make him red, with horns and stuff, but I just wanted him to look like an ordinary sailor.

"If we just draw a sailor, nobody will know who it's supposed to be," Jesse said.

"They will," I practically shrieked.

Jesse glowered and said, "This is stupid kid's stuff anyway. This is why we never get any chicks, because you're still into stupid kid's stuff."

"How can it be kid's stuff? Comic books are all written and illustrated by adults," I said.

"'Comic books are all written and illustrated by adults,'" he mocked. "No wonder people think we're dorks. It's because of you."

I wondered if that was true. Maybe Jesse could hang out with the cool kids and drink beer with chicks if it wasn't for me. I erased hard and the paper started to pill. It didn't matter. Jesse couldn't get the arms right anyway.

We stayed up late and watched the eleven o'clock news with mom and dad. Mom bitched about getting an air conditioner.

"Dave Nelson, you're a cheap bastard," she said to dad. Which was funny because she was the one into ecology and all that stuff, and dad called her a hypocrite and then she couldn't think of anything else to say to that.

"Men always win arguments because of their superior logic," dad said and mom swatted him.

The news was still all about the oil spill. "Newtown Creek is the most polluted body of water in the world," they said, "followed by the Gowanus Canal."

"The Go-anus Canal," Jesse called it.

"Go to bed or I'll sign you up for computer camp," dad said.

I still wanted to play Sailor, but Jesse got mad and told me to shut up and go to sleep.

But it was way too hot to sleep. I tossed around for a bit, then got up around quarter to four. Jesse was gone.

"Jess," I whispered.

I opened the window to the fire escape. He wasn't out there. The street was quiet. It was almost cool outside, there was a little breath of freshness to the air. He went to the creek, I realized. ("How did you know?" they would ask me later. I can't say how I knew. I just did.) I wondered if he went there with beers and girls. I imagined him meeting girls out on the street, being cool, going to the corner deli where, in my fantasy, they didn't care about ID, and taking them to the creek.

I followed him.

The barriers were still unguarded and the police tape was mostly torn away; everything looked abandoned and bombed-out, like a war movie.

"Jess, you here?" I called softly. Silence.

I saw a metal shell on the ground -- it looked like a shell anyway. Shrapnel. I kicked it and started messing around, pretending I was on the battlefield. "Sh-ttt-tt," I made the sound effects of a machine gun. "G-sh!" A grenade going off. The shore was a minefield. I took cover by an iron girder, ducking behind it to keep an eye on the imaginary V.C. who darted among the crates and industrial cartons the size of dumpsters.

And yet they *were* there. Something was there. I heard a shuffling and muffled breath as someone ran from one crate to another. There was the brief flash of a fleeing form, and then nothing.

And then I heard it again.

I was definitely not alone.

I crept along the length of the shore, listening to the scraping of feet and ragged breathing. I couldn't tell if he was beside me or behind me, but I knew that he was there. My arms windmilled as I tried to find him in the darkness and my foot slipped a little on some loose shale by the pilings. I pulled my foot back from the edge, and then I saw them.

Jesse. And the man from my dream.

Jesse stood a little ways down the shore, staring down into the creek. The man stood behind him; up close he was scrawny and even more ragged and dirty than I'd realized.

He turned his face slowly toward me. It was scabrous, infested, hollow and gaunt. His mouth was open; the eyes that fixed on me were the eyes of a madman.

"Get away from him! Jesse get away from him!" I screamed.

Jesse looked all around. "Who?"

The man lunged into the water, grabbing Jesse.

By the time I got to where they'd been standing, the thick bubbles in the surface of the filthy water had almost stopped burbling. I dropped to my knees to look; there was nothing but darkness. They were gone. Somewhere down there Jesse was choking on oil, pollution lacerating his skin, and I had brought this on him.

And that's when I lit the creek on fire.

I watched as the water began to glow with low blue flames. It looked like a TV flickering. One match, a small blue flame. Another match, a brighter glow. Another match, another match, another match. More and more, brighter and brighter, the water changing from blue to red. I could see him down there, floating, one pale arm reaching thinly up through the water – but no, the water was black. I saw nothing. I remember nothing. I don't remember what I saw. His eyes, red – no, I saw nothing. I did not see the ragged man again, he was gone, his burning eyes were all burned up, and nothing but flame remained.

It is strange that I had matches in my pocket. I don't remember bringing them.

The sun had started to rise by the time I got home and mom and dad were freaking out. "I went to look for Jesse," I told them, and they looked at each other with panicked eyes.

We called the police and they dredged the creek but I knew it was too late. By that time Jesse would be incinerated, cremated, dissipated by the chemical stew. Police and reporters swarmed around our building and Mom cried a lot. "Why did you do it?" she kept asking. "Why did you go down there?"

I kept trying to tell her -- he went there first.

The police asked me a bunch of questions. "Did your brother go down here?" they asked. "I don't know." "Why did you come here last night?" "I was looking for him." "Did he say he was planning to come here?" "No." "Why did you come to the bridge?" "I don't know."

I heard them muttering to themselves. "Dredging the fucking canal and the fucking canal's on fire."

"It's not a canal, it's a creek," I said.

"What?"

"Nothing."

I was watching *Knight Rider* when I saw mom and dad talking about me in the kitchen. I know what they were talking about because they kept looking over at me.

That night I worked on the comic book, adding a prologue about why Kristos Bustos looked like an ordinary sailor (you know why it is now, Jesse – didn't I tell you?). I decided I was going to make him the main character. The comic book is my work of art now. I can create the characters, I can destroy them.

Clive is the only person I tell. Clive understands things better than 99% of people I know. We're working on the comic together. He just colors and traces because he can't draw but he never argues with me about the story and he still laughs at all my jokes. I'm starting to get attached to Clive. And his parents are pleased that I am with him. He spent so much time alone, they said.

THE END

"Do you know who that was?" asked Grace, after the silvery-haired woman had left.

"Who?" Chris barely looked up from his book.

"Joan Hassell. I thought so when I saw Joan H. on the chalkboard, and now I know it. I recognize her from her author photos."

"Are you going to ask for her autograph?"

"Don't be silly."

Grace and Christopher had arrived the night before. It had been raining – a foggy, pernicious coastal drizzle – and the old house was dimly lit.

In the front hallway they saw a chalkboard with four names written on it, each name followed by an initial: Joan H., Lisa D., Mallory M., Grace S.

Chris had laughed. "They're all girls' names."

"At a quaint bed and breakfast by the seashore? Shocker."

In the light of morning, Grace waited impatiently to go to the beach – Chris had been leafing through *A History of Montauk* since they finished breakfast nearly an hour ago – when the silvery-haired woman walked into the room, or rather, *glided*. She had a pretentious, self-conscious way of moving that announced itself by saying, "Don't look at me."

Grace said shyly, "Hello."

The woman glanced at her and returned the greeting with the cautious defensiveness of celebrity. She turned her gaze to the books on the shelf, sweeping her eyes over the paperbacks.

Grace, rather embarrassingly, jumped up from her seat. "Try this one," handing her Josephine Tey's *The Franchise Affair*. The woman regarded it with an odd smile. "What kind of book is it?"

"A mystery."

The woman turned it over in her hands. "Oh? Maybe I'll give it a try." There was something curious about the expression on her face. She seemed to find the presence of the tattered volume inordinately amusing.

Suddenly Grace was embarrassed. (*This is Joan fucking Hassell; of course she's read it before.*) She blushed and lowered her gaze, then shifted it over to the window. Outside, the hot, clear sky shimmered over a blue sea – the kind of summer scene that seduces editorial assistants to spend half a month's rent on a weekend in the Hamptons.

(Grace and Chris had felt like interlopers when they came downstairs that morning and saw the other guests already eating breakfast. They had hesitated, unsure of how to proceed. Should they help themselves from the breakfast table strewn with sticky jam jars and half-opened packages of English muffins? Or did they wait to be served?

Grace noticed that one of the guests, a little boy with dark hair cut in a shaggy Eton crop, had been staring at them.

"My name's Mila," the child finally said.

Mila. She was a girl. Grace looked at her. Her small, pointed face and narrow eyes looked rather wizened and elfin, and seemed to carry a look of profound skepticism.

"Have you ever been to a beach before?" asked Mila.

"Yes, lots of times."

"You'd better watch out, the waves here are really big."

"Thanks for the warning. I'll be careful!" Grace widened her eyes in exaggerated fright. Mila's skeptical look remained.

"Never turn your back on a wave," she said.)

Grace was so lost in thought she didn't realize the silvery-haired woman was still talking to her.

"Are you a mystery fan?" she repeated.

"I like all the canonical stuff," stuttered Grace. "Conan Doyle, the usual. Poe, of course." (*Canonical. Ugh.*)

"Mmm. Poe gets a lot of credit for inventing the detective story. Of course, he was predated by Ann Radcliff."

"Really?"

"Mm-hm. Emily St. Aubert was an amateur detective in her own way. Without her we wouldn't have Dupin, Holmes, or Miss Marple. The genre simply wouldn't exist."

Grace didn't want to admit she didn't know who Emily St. Aubert was, so she said tentatively, "I've heard rumors that your next book will be your last Inspector Rector mystery. Is it true?"

"Well, I hate to spread rumors, but perhaps there is a chance that I'm ready to move on. After seventeen years and thirty novels, don't you think it's time we lay Rector to rest?"

"I suppose so. I mean, that makes sense."

The woman smiled at her, more warmly than before.

"Are you a writer, too?"

(Of course I am. We're the only ones who read any more.)

"Yes."

"Well, it really is nice to meet another writer. We get so many of them here. At least one comes up every summer."

"Joan, let's go." A tall, fit-looking man in his seventies loomed into view and took the woman gently by the arm. He looked like he played tennis every day and starred in vitamin advertisements. Together they gave off an air of robustly preserved good health.

Joan wrapped a towel around her slim, almost androgynous, body. "Well," she said, "I'm off to brave the surf." She smiled at Grace and walked away with her companion.

* * *

"Yup, she's definitely Joan Hassell."

The beach was across the street, accessible from a narrow pathway that cut through a green tangle of bramble and dune grass. Chris underestimated the sharpness of the grass until a blade sliced into him. "That's bush league," he said, blood trickling from his foot.

"Chris," said Grace absently as they picked their way among the dunes, "Did you notice the scars by her ears?"

"No."

"She has tiny scars, like from a facelift. She's definitely had work done."

"I'm sure she has."

"I wonder how old she is."

"Hmm," said Chris, limping.

The surf was as rough as Mila had forewarned.

"I've never seen it like this!" Grace exclaimed, laughing. Chris looked nervous. They cavorted in the sea for as long as they could bear it but eventually relented, breathlessly pounded into submission by the wall of white water. It was impossible to get beyond the breakers and truly swim, so they sat on the sand in the searing sun until they could stand no more.

* * *

Grace was starting to hate this place. She'd been sitting on the porch for the last half-hour, bored and staring jealously at the sprawling family-style motel next door, with its rather immense swimming pool. *You had to choose the "quaint" place, you sucker.*

Chris had declined to sit and read on the porch with her. "You're not coming with?" she'd asked.

He held up the remote. "Yankees game."

"Fine."

The sun was setting, but Grace couldn't see it since it was on the other side of the island. Her pen rested idly upon her notebook, atop a blank page. She sat there until all was dark except for the moon slowly rising. There was something about the emptiness of the countryside, something about the silence broken only by surprisingly noisy crickets that gave her the unpleasant sensation of being watched. By the time she left the porch, she had written a single word in her notebook: crickets.

* * *

"Grace. Do come in."

The door to Room Number One was ajar. Joan sat with her companion, who waved her in.

"Share a smoke?"

"Should I close the door?"

"Oh, nobody minds."

"Sure."

Grace couldn't believe it. *Smoking pot with Joan Hassell!* She looked around the room as though trying to commit the moment to memory. She ran her eyes over the mess of clothes on the floor and wet towels strewn thoughtlessly over wooden chairs. A laptop lay on the bed and a lot of very expensive-looking leather luggage was scattered about the room. A small wooden box rested atop the dresser. It looked antique and was made of what appeared to be ivory. It was ornately carved with what seemed, to Grace's untrained eye, to be designs of vaguely African origins; beneath them was a date: 1795. It was quite a fancy place to keep a stash. *I should go get Chris*, she thought. And then her eyes fell on something that made her reconsider: a manuscript.

With horror, Grace recognized it as one of her short stories. A particularly shitty one she'd brought with her to edit on the train. *I will absolutely kill him.* Chris always said her biggest problem was one of self-promotion. They had to make friends in the literary scene, he said – ironically aspirating that word, "scene" – though they never did anything at parties and book launches but stand to the side and talk to one another.

She picked up the flimsy sheaf of paper. "Oh my gosh, Joan, I'm so sorry. I can't believe he gave that to you."

"Don't be. You're not bad."

"Really?"

"Well, there is room for improvement, of course, but you're certainly… adequate."

Adequate! *Gee, thanks lady.*

And then something else caught Grace's eye. A bit of plastic sheeting was poking out from behind the bed, the kind you get at the dry cleaners. Actually, lots of plastic sheeting, yards of it heaped in a pile beneath the bed. *That's a hell of a lot of dry-cleaning*, she thought.

The room had become silent. Joan was staring at her. Even in the darkness, Grace could see that something metallic gleamed in the author's hand.

"I gotta go," she said.

Grace left the room but never made it back up the stairs.

As she walked through the front room, her legs felt less and less steady. She sat down heavily on the edge of the sofa. Yesterday's books still lay on the coffee table, only now something seemed different about them. "The History of Montauk" was now "A History of Haiti." She shook her head. That didn't seem right.

"What are you doing here?"

Mila stood behind her, black eyes glinting in the dark. With her shaggy hair and luminous pupils, she looked just like a little raccoon caught pawing through somebody's garbage cans.

"Just resting."

Grace hated being stoned in front of children. It seemed so indecent.

"It's raining again," Mila said and walked away.

Grace exhaled. She really was way too stoned. Something didn't feel right. She was numb and dizzy.

Somewhere, laughter echoed – laughter and voices. Mila and... someone else, someone with a deeper register. A man. Grace listened, but the voices seemed to be fading into the distance.

Joan's companion loomed into view. "Come, my dear, you're ready. Come." Grace acquiesced. Standing very close to him, she noticed he, too, had the scars behind his ears. He caught her looking. "Cosmetic surgery wasn't always so sophisticated as it is now," he smiled.

He took her to Joan's room. He lay her down on the bed, which was encased in the plastic sheeting. Joan stood at the side of the bed, towering over her.

"What's happening?" Grace murmured drowsily. She felt her eyes fluttering and tried desperately to focus on Joan, who leaned down and caressed her face. Her hands were as cold as the bottom of the sea. Grace shivered and Joan laughed cruelly. Her eyes flickered, enlivened by a strange light.

"Come, Joan, quickly now – prepare the girl," her companion said. "While she's still alive."

"Yes, my dear. Sit up Grace; I want to show you something. Sit up."

Grace was limp; Joan had to maneuver her into a sitting position and hoist her up to standing. Her legs buckled and she staggered as Joan practically dragged her over to a small closet in the corner of the room. She stood there, swaying, her knees dipping down toward the earth as Joan forced her head up. "Look!" she rasped. "What do you see?" Joan's spindly thumbs propped her eyes open.

The image swam before her but soon came into focus. Books. Nothing but books – shelves of them.

"I see…" Grace couldn't remember the word for *books*. "Them."

"Mine. All mine!"

"She doesn't understand, Ann," her companion said.

("Ann?" thought Grace.)

"You see, little Grace, this is my glory, my greatest project. I wrote them all – every single word in these pages, all of it belongs to me – I perfected the form, you know, and it can never really be equaled by anyone else."

These books were not Inspector Rector mysteries – or at least they didn't look like them. Grace couldn't be sure of anything anymore, but these were not the fat paperbacks with the embossed spines she was used to. She reached for one, numbly.

"Yes, that's my girl. You want to look at them, don't you?" Joan thrust one into Grace's hands. Grace swayed unsteadily, concentrating furiously on the title of the thick leather volume. *The Mysteries of the Forest* by Ann Radcliffe, it said.

"You didn't write this." Grace mumbled thickly.

"Says who?"

(He called her "Ann.")

"No. No… too old."

"1791… a good year."

Grace just shook her head. No, no, no. Vigorously shaking.

"It always takes them a while to figure it out. You seem to be a little duller than the rest…" Joan shot a look at her companion – "Darling, I really worry a bit about this brain, you know" – then put her face very close to Grace. "I'll spell it out for you. Since the clock is ticking on your inadequate little cerebrum."

Joan jabbed her finger at the books on the shelf. "Ann Radcliffe, Edgar Poe, Conan Doyle, Agatha Christie! I wrote them all!"

"You'r'a... liar."

Joan slapped her, but Grace hardly felt it.

"You little idiot, you couldn't understand."

Joan grabbed *The Mysteries of Udolpho* and opened it to a well-worn page. "*'She had passed the spring of youth, but her wit prolonged the triumph of its reign, and they mutually assisted the fame of each other...'*"

Her companion interjected. "It isn't worth telling her, Ann."

"I suppose not. Look at her gaping. Have you figured it out yet, child? Of course she hasn't! Come *bokor*, let us begin!"

Bokor? Grace didn't know the word.

"It's a voodoo priest, you simp," Joan snapped. ("Did I say that out loud?" Grace wondered.) "He's the one who came to me with a proposal in the last years of our eighteenth century. How would you like to live forever, Annie? How would you like to write and write and never stop? Never feel the ideas fade away! Never feel your power wane! To be revered and celebrated... A little 'voudou' trick picked up among Caribbean slaves, tested on them, guaranteed to work. The poison is willfully ingested, but *controlled*, you see! Everything in just the right dosage, just the right amount – like the anesthesia his colleagues would eventually begin to understand."

"It isn't simply a matter of ingesting the substance," her companion said. "It all comes down to the right proportions in the toxins and, of course, to timing. And eating the brain of another writer, naturally. My dear, if you will."

Joan moved Grace over to the bed. "Down you go, little chicken."

Suddenly, Grace grabbed her wrist. "Wait – wait – is this true? Really true?"

"Why would I lie?"

"But... Poe? Doesn't make... sense... he'ss'a... man..."

"Should I happen to possess the characteristics of both Hermes and Aphrodite, is that any reason to discriminate against me?"

"But you look... not... like him."

"It's amazing what you can do if you only have enough... skin." She flicked her finger against Grace's cheek, which elicited not even a wince.

"She is ready," said the *bokor*.

Grace felt the blade of a knife-like instrument cutting into her skull. *(A scalpel, that's what it's called.)* That was the metallic thing she'd seen gleaming in Joan's hand before.

Grace managed to gasp out a weak "please-no."

"No?" said Ann. "Don't you see, my little poppet, this might be your only chance…" Her mouth curved sardonically. "Haven't you always wanted to *become* a writer?"

It became difficult to see when the blood began streaming into her eyes, but there was no doubt of what was happening. Ann and her *bokor* used knives and forks to gouge out parts of Grace's pulsating brain and ate them with great delicacy.

"Well, she put up less of a fuss than Josephine bloody Tey did," the esteemed authoress remarked.

"She's passing over, Ann," the *bokor* said.

"Ann," whispered Grace.

"I was never out of print, you know," she said soothingly, taking another mincing bite of cerebellum. "Not for two hundred years."

Things began to go dark for Grace; that is to say, darker.

"You have a very lovely face," Ann said. "I look forward to wearing it."

She turned to her companion and *bokor*, and smiled. "To another hundred stories."

"To another hundred years."

MORBUS

"That's right, Morton, you son of a bitch, pack it in!"

I watch from across the street as the servants shove trunks into a landau. The rich pukes are going away to their country manors in the Hudson Valley, leaving the city to the likes of me. I keep my hat down close over my eyes as I watch them leave. I don't want anyone to recognize me when I come up here later, when their houses are shuttered and empty, for that's when I smash and grab.

Morton – Morton, the man whose wealth towers above all others! "Strikebreaker!" the headlines call him. His carriages clatter down Fifth Avenue and whisk his family away, one of dozens who've fled the heat and plague of Manhattan's miasmatic summer swamp, leaving behind a ghost town that is simply *full* of treasure.

But before I make my move I must await the sunset. Home I go, to pass the time in a dark room with a cup of something cool.

I live in the dwelling known as the Rookery, jammed in with the scum of the sixth ward. The Rookery is a warren, its tunnels burrowing into Stygian gloom where "rum-degraded human beings" (as old Dickens himself called us) vie with vermin for a place to sleep amid the rags and dirt. We live in the shadow of City Hall, which only seems to enhance our predilection for corruption. All manner of degenerates cram into rooms fifteen feet square; thieves, murderers, pickpockets, beggars and harlots eke out a living in these abject dens, vice their only mode of income – for in common they share a loathing for labor – and quench their insatiable thirst for ale, porter, malt and beer in the makeshift taverns hidden behind false-fronted dry goods stores.

I happen to loathe the place. I am not a degenerate, nor am I a thief by nature – merely by trade. It is only unfortunate circumstance that thrusts me here among these people; I don't deserve to be here, as they do. I've seen better things and I will return to better things. I've lived in the countryside and know its fresh green pleasures, pleasures of which these wretched denizens of urban squalor are entirely ignorant. I used to live near a forest of pines as a lad. They worked me hard on the farm and I ran away, but I never forgot the soft sound of wind sighing in the pines, or the blessed scent of it, a scent I try to bring to mind when the noisome city oppresses me. But a man cannot be a country gentleman without means.

I watch them now from the corner of my eye as I sit alone with my drink; I try to shut out the sounds of laughter and screaming and shattering glass as they intoxicate themselves. One of them coughs and I shudder. There have been many illnesses this summer.

Every year the pestilence comes, from June to August, as though taking a holiday from Hades. It likes to summer in the slums, delighting in ravaging the poor. The broken-down constitutions of these miserable creatures succumb almost instantly on the attack. Disease, I thank you, for purging the very dross of the city! Let these dissolute and filthy people die huddled together like pigs in their self-made sties!

One of them screams now, with terror or delight I cannot tell. "Why screaming?" I wonder. I myself am in the habit of raising a glass of gin and am not possessed with the desire to shriek and scream – why are they? There is always one with a voice much louder than the rest, usually a woman, whose conversation floats above all others. The shrill female voice hits me like a slap to the face. There are no peaceful evenings because of them. I cannot sleep or walk unmolested in the street; they are everywhere, like flies on a pile of shit.

There isn't a man I've ever met whom I don't secretly think a fool. There isn't a single person in all this great wide world I want to share it with, except maybe Claire Bliss, the girl who tends bar in the tavern. But even Claire, for all her angel face, had been with dozens of men and was said to have a fair bit of trouble from it downstairs.

I suppose the gist of it is I never really cared for human beings in general, be they rich or poor. But in this case, it was a rich man who was going to help me out.

The idea came to me when I found a ragged old copy of the *Daily Times* in Bliss' bar. Claire never had much in the way of reading material at her establishment, and I can't think which of the neighborhood illiterates would have left it there, but in any case, something in it caught my eye: an article on the financier Morton, known not only as the richest man in New York, if not America, but the most singularly influential, bending and shaping the country's fiscal policy to his own needs and will, the kind of man who could collapse and destroy an entire nation's economy without qualm or consequence – to his vast fortune, anyway. He was one of those very clever types who seemed to have an infinite capacity for getting richer while the rest of the country got poorer, the only man on earth who could make over a million by closing a factory. "Latest expenditures raise ire among workers," the headlines said.

Now this was something.

Morton was beginning to gain a reputation among the ink-slingers of the country, who relished writing about his beloved library. The man, it seemed, was obsessed with filling it with the world's rarest, most expensive and most important books and manuscripts, a monument to his ego, furnished by pillage. He'd also bought a great deal of antique statuary, and this was what interested me. "Adds Roman knickknacks to growing collection of ancient detritus," the paper told me, "Several small solid-gold statues shipped to his upper Fifth Avenue estate."

"What are you doing with that? That's a Republican paper," Claire spat.

Bless her, she didn't know a thing about politics but she was loyal to whoever bought her vote.

I became obsessed with Morton's wealth. The injustice of it crowded my mind, made me grind my teeth while I slept, dreaming of my own hate, awaking with blinding headaches. The headaches descended with a nauseating, hallucinatory pain. At first I tried to lie down and let them pass, but then I learned to ride the waves of searing agony, letting them wash over me and lift me up the boulevard to Morton's massive marble estate, like a raft floating on a river current. It was there, standing across the street from his estate, mud from the half-finished park wetting my shoes, that I realized he would be the one to finance my exodus.

The sun is setting now and I make my way quietly to the white shining mansions of Fifth Avenue, jewels glittering in the moonshine. I have watched and counted the servants and know there is one man left on the premises, and one girl; both have Saturday nights off. Saturday night is a fine night to work; everyone else is too busy with his own pleasure to notice you quietly toiling. A man may work uninterrupted, and in secret.

I bring my knife with me, just in case, though I know both servants leave by eight o'clock. One never knows when there might be an unexpected early return, and one cannot be too safe.

The servants' quarters are always the best way to enter any big house. The gate is locked with a simple device that I make short work of. Once inside the grounds I find the lock on their door laughably easy to penetrate. Their quarters are separated from the main house by another locked door this one, however, much more complicated. Vastly more complicated. It takes me over a half hour's work to break it, thinking the whole time of Morton's family gamboling on the soaring banks of the Hudson, white-clad girls playing lawn tennis by the glittering blue water, young men lounging in the shade in straw hats, cicadas chirping, servants bringing them cucumber sandwiches in the cool of evening.

By the time I pick the lock I am hot and thirsty and my head has begun to throb dully. No matter, for soon I will be away from the city, and then, no doubt, once removed from the pestilential polis, will recover.

The main house is hushed, quiet and dark, and I let my eyes adjust to the dim light for a moment so I can take in the splendor around me. Some criticize him for his taste, call it vulgar, but I admire the way he buys what he pleases. I also rather admire myself for stealing it.

The heat has penetrated the dark drapes and sealed windows and it feels like a hot stove in the main entryway, despite the surfeit of marble décor. My scuff-soled shoes don't make much in the way of noise on that floor so I poke around pretty recklessly. I find the library quickly, as though by instinct. Richly paneled in mahogany, draped in wine-dark damask – the works. Just as the papers said. I reflect again how foolhardy he has been, letting the whole world know where he keeps his goods.

His oil portrait hangs over the fireplace, a massive, highly flattering rendering. Directly beneath this monstrosity is assembled a rich collection of gold figurines. All quite ancient looking, all undoubtedly insured and very recognizable. But, luckily for me, all eminently melt-able. A good fence should be able to turn them into bricks in no time. Into the bag they go.

What next? There are books and maps, dozens of them, but what kind of ready cash would they bring? I help myself to more gold. The heat in the library seems even worse than that woodstove of a hallway and I work up a fierce sweat. I wish I could pause in my thirsty work. I grab a bronze figurine and make to throw it in the sack but something stops me. The eyes are made of rubies and flash like fire even in the dim light. It's quite arresting and I can't help but gaze at it for a moment. It's a queer little figure: shaped like a man, with a bent and crooked frame and a bulbous nose placed square in the middle of a large, bald head. It bears a funny resemblance to the Man himself, though not the oil painting version of himself. I throw it in.

I cough a little and wish for a second time I had something to drink. A decanter resting on a small cabinet catches my eye. Perhaps a drink of something expensive will restore me. I quaff deeply of an excellent sherry. Thus restored, I look around the room for my final sweep. Very little left glitters gold or bronze. I am finished here, unless I can think very quickly of a place where Himself might keep a healthy stash of bank notes. For good measure I plunder the desk drawers finding nothing but stamps and seals and heavy stationery. I look once more to the shelves. Treasures, bah! Nothing but a lot of old books. That's it for my haul. I spit on the floor, take my knife from my jacket and with one really satisfying rip, tear a massive hole in the crimson damask adorning the walls.

I am preparing my exit from the library when suddenly it descends: the old headache. I groan and instinctively grab my temple. The bag falls to the floor and I crouch to retrieve it. I find, once down, that I can't get up: I am quite literally doubled-over in pain, incapacitated. Indescribable agony! My left temple feels as though I'd been smashed with a wooden mallet, my teeth feel as though I'd been grinding glass. My left eye throbs and a fork of lightning sears my face with shooting pain. I lie there, grasping desperately for my bag of plunder. I have my hands on it but can't hold it; they're too weak. My god, why can't I get up!

A clarion sound rings out from somewhere. It makes me stop what I'm doing to listen. Ding! Ding! Whence does it come, and what is it? A whimsical clock chiming the hour? It sounds like a little child ringing a silver bell. There is a sweetness to the sound, an almost unbearable sweetness – its pitch is so high, the ringing interminable. It sounds like a tuning fork, really, more than a bell, and the reverberation seems infinite.

The sound increases in pitch, becomes unbearable. Pain radiates throughout my entire body. It chokes me, clenching and tightening the back of my throat. This is by far the worst yet but somehow I manage to hoist myself up to my knees and then, finally, stagger to my feet. It feels as though my head is splitting in two – and then I catch sight of myself in a gilt-edged mirror and see exactly *why* I feel that way.

My head, it seems, *is* splitting in two.

One half of my skull leans to the left, the other veers to the right. And then a man, fully-formed, and fully armed, leaps from the crevice between the two lobes of my brain and lands on the parquet floor.

He is wretchedly thin, with a jaundiced tinge to his complexion, eyes sunken and parched, skin drawn tightly over a bony skull. He extends his hands to me, claw-like, and I shudder. It might be my imagination but he looks a little hurt when I do that.

"What are you?" I manage to gasp.

"You know, my friend. Or you shall, soon. That's a rather glaring hole in your skull, isn't it? Unseemly. Let's fix that."

Incredible – I run my hands over my head and it is just as it had been. Whole! Surely I am hallucinating.

"No blood," say I, disbelieving.

"Is there supposed to be?" asks the man, with the tone of one inquiring politely about the weather. "Was that not typical of such cases? I'm not sure what the regular symptoms of a head splitting in two are."

I don't really pay attention to his words just then; I'm distracted by my wrenching stomach cramps. I double over, and reacquaint myself with the floor. As I lie there prone and immobilized I notice I have a punishing thirst, perhaps as a result of the brandy I'd drunk. But worst of all were the cramps.

"My guts!"

"A mere trifle compared to what's going to happen now. Quite a lot will start happening to your body all at once. I'm afraid this will be rather uncomfortable. I might as well sit down for this; it often takes several hours."

And damned if he doesn't grab an armchair and make himself at home. He's right, though: what happens next is powerfully uncomfortable, and embarrassing. A large wet pool appears on the rug beneath me. I seem to be leaking several fluids all at once.

"No, No!" I cry. "This isn't real, this is a trick of the mind!"

"Is it?"

"It's a trick of the heat!"

"How stubborn you are." The man sighs. "You must think it odd that I've attacked only your friends in the Rookery and not —"

"Friends!" I cry. "Intemperate swine!"

"You're no temperance man yourself."

"I'm not one of *them*."

"Ah, so you are like Morton then? A wealthy man?"

"Not… yet…" I say with difficulty, through clenched teeth. "Soon enough."

"And yet you can't seem to stand up on your own. Odd, for such a powerful man, poised on the cusp of wealth."

How that enrages me! I am feverish with hate for this man-creature before me and steel myself to get up and go at him with my knife. He notices my efforts, evidently, for he redoubles his offensive. The surface of my body burns with fever, and the great pain in my head crashes over me in a fresh wave.

"Most men would have asked me who I am by now," he said.

"I know who you are, you're a fever and you'll go away just as soon as I get my strength back."

He smirks. "Hot dry skin, stiff to the touch? Ah yes, that would seem to describe you right now, friend."

"I'm not your friend." I spit. "And I'm getting tired of you."

"I'll tell you who I am, since you won't deign to ask. I am the demon they call Morbus, brother to Pestis and Dolor."

"Never heard of 'em."

This seems to irk him. He snarls nastily. "How goes the cramping and clenching of your bowels? The nausea? The evacuation of fluids?" The demon laughs to himself and rubs his hands together in glee. "How goes the blinding pain in your head? Such an amusing way to kill – "

"So that's what you want, eh? To kill me? All right, go ahead and get it over with!"

The Demon ignores me and begins to wander through the library, examining the various objects and rifling through books. He pauses when he comes to the Gutenberg bible, open on its display stand, and makes a distasteful face. "I don't care much for this book. Ever since it came along people assume I'm that Satan fellow, which I think is preposterous. How can one demon get all the evil in the world done alone, I ask you?" He pauses contemplatively under Morton's portrait and sighs. "Though I wouldn't mind hanging around to watch the fun old Satan's going to have with *him* one day."

I start to sob, only I'm so thoroughly dried out that the sobs merely manifest themselves as dry, wracking little heaves. The demon clucks his tongue – I do believe he feels sorry for me! – and asks me what's wrong. I can't explain myself, I only say, "My country house!"

"Ah yes, this house in the country you so desire! Have you even inquired as to whether there was real estate available? Where exactly you plan to live? Have you figured on having enough cash to live on long after you buy it? I have to say I don't quite think you've thoroughly thought this thing through. You're no J.P Morton, I can tell you! That man is a mastermind!

These new men of business, they outdo even us, I tell you! No, son, you are no capitalist. If you were, you'd be at your country house already and I would have spared you. Alas, I'm afraid your lot is with the intemperate swine."

He stares at me for a moment, then snaps his fingers. I begin vomiting violently.

"That's better. I'd like to speed this up. You're rather depressing me, I'm afraid. I can stand anything except self-pity."

And unless my eyes are playing tricks on me, I swear he reaches into the folds of his black robe and takes out a pocket watch, which he glances at with a sigh.

I relent a little. "What's happening to me?"

"In medical terms, your body is shutting down. You are losing all your water. In layman's terms, you are submitting to the dangers of August. In cosmic terms, you are fulfilling your natural destiny."

His speechifying is starting to wear on my nerves. If this cramping ever stops I'm going to take my knife and gut this fellow.

But he has more for me: "First there will be a reduction of blood in your body. Your heart will pump harder to try to keep it flowing but to no avail." He flourishes a bit of faded, yellowed newspaper, clears his throat and grins. "As they wrote of my handiwork in the *Times*: 'While the mechanism of life is suddenly arrested, the body will be emptied by a few rapid gushes of its serum, and reduced to a damp, dead mass.' Beautifully phrased, isn't it? And true! Meanwhile, the mind remains untouched and clear so you will be aware of every organ shutting down, a 'spirit looking out in terror from a corpse.' Oh I *do* love that!"

"Hardly seems… like I got a… clear mind." My talk is reduced to a stammer as I void my bowels all over Morgan's god-damned rug again. It sounds like someone pouring water out a second-story window.

"Your face," he replies, ignoring my embarrassment, "is a beautiful shade of blue."

I touch it; it feels like leather.

He looks at me contemplatively, and begins muttering to himself as though making notes. "Countenance quite shrunk, eyes sunk, lips dark blue. Nails livid."

He chuckles.

"Though I dislike you, I do enjoy my work. Nothing makes it easier than you humans! Your folly is nearly incomprehensible! You haven't got a clue how to stop me. Did I ever tell you about my greatest moment, in London in 1665? The aldermen actually thought it was dogs and cats that were causing the plague so they ordered them all killed! And the whole time it was" – here he laughs so hard he doubles over and can hardly finish his sentence – "it was the *rats*!"

He finished chuckling and wiped the tears from his eyes.

I don't see what's so funny. Frankly, things are starting to feel a little, well, blurry. Slowly I feel myself begin to drift in and out of consciousness. At one point the demon goes over to the door and locks it.

"You don't want to be found by a servant, do you? That would be most demeaning. They won't come into this room if it's locked, they never do. They haven't the temerity."

At least I think that's what he says; frankly, I'm paying slightly less attention to the demon now, and more to my various bodily tortures, though I think I see the demon help himself to some brandy at some point in the seemingly interminable night.

Finally, finally, it is dawn and I am thoroughly desiccated. I lie on the floor and draw my last breath, brittle paper skin crackling as I open my mouth. I have completely ruined the rug. The demon stands over me one last time. He leans down and very gently kisses my forehead. He kicks my bag away from my hand and whispers: "What world does money belong to? This world. What world does a dead man belong to? 'Tother world."

I deeply regret the loss of my bag of gold.

The demon says, "Sorry to have to do you in this way, but it *is* August, and for everything there is a season, so they say. I think I'll go back to the Rookery now, for it's far too empty uptown."

MORNING ALL DAY

"But it hasn't got a fireplace."

Fred goes pale, then red, at these words, and seems to choke down a retort he knows could never be taken back once loosed upon the world. I say "I'm sorry but it's true," but I'm not really sorry. I don't see why I should have to give up my personal standards and live in a sterile, ugly, modern box! Those white cubicles stacked like shoeboxes in mid-town! I'm telling you now, I refuse to do it.

And yet it seems that Fred has reached the end of his fraying tether, so I don't say any more, for now. Mentally I gird myself for another wearisome day of apartment-hunting, wondering what fresh horrors await me on the morrow, what new abominations I will see as I survey the leaky lay of the landlord. A bubble of resentment simmers and pops inside me at the thought of it. It's not as though I'm the only one who wants to move! Fred's just as eager to go as I am, and yet all the house hunting seems to fall under my exclusive jurisdiction somehow. As though I have nothing better to think about. Between my poetry, singing and acting I hardly have time for anything. I imagine Fred thinks I was a woman of leisure just because I don't run a restaurant all day.

I peek at Fred over a folded corner of newspaper and watch him sullenly poking the fire. I can't imagine not having one roaring in the autumn evenings as the cool wind sweeps down West Tenth Street any more than I can imagine seeing office buildings outside my window instead of the charming chimney pots of the Village. I'm certainly not going to hurry this move just because he all of a sudden decided it's time. I've been begging him to move out for years, and now that he was ready, it's all rush, rush, rush! Well he can just sit tight. It wasn't as if he was the one sleeping on the recamier – he's safely ensconced in the bedroom, where the specters dare not venture. I'm the one who suffers every night beneath the archway, on the daybed, watching their vile shadows loom over me in the wee hours!

I dig my hand into Tessa's silken fur, grateful for her soft, stable breathing. If it hadn't been for her, Fred would never have believed me. The night she stood opposite the blue wing chair, growling, hackles raised, haunches stiff, backing slowly away – it wasn't until then that Fred finally saw what I'd been seeing all along. We watched her as she followed the spirit with her canny canine gaze; the thing, whatever you want to call it, seemed to move from the chair, through the archway, and, hovering around my mini-grand, settle on the recamier – I knew it! – and stay there. That's where Tessa's sightline settled, too; that's where she stood and growled until the whites of her eyes were visible, until foam formed furiously at the corners of her mouth.

"There, do you see it!?" I'd screamed, shaking him by the collar. "Do you see it now?"

He looked at me then looked at Tessa. Back and forth between us as though deciding who to believe. Finally he said, "We're moving."

He had doubted me; oh how he had doubted me. He laughed when I wrote my letter of entreaty to Hans Holzer. I will admit he was right about Holzer; his promised thaumaturgy turned out to be a fraud of the first order. But what of all the other signs? The very first night we moved in, I saw the shadow loom over the bed. It swept over me and I felt something brush my face. There was something unspeakably sinister in it that left me sleepless, hands trembling as I lit innumerable cigarettes and waited until dawn. "A bird flying over the moon," he told me. A bird indeed!

Fred now claims he said an airplane, not a bird. "If an object comes between a light source and the surface it is projecting on, it will cast a shadow," he explained with condescending false patience. "An airplane flying over the moon, a cloud passing, a kid tossing a basketball in the air beside a streetlight – anything." Bird, plane, Superman, it doesn't matter. I know what I saw.

I was so completely unstrung after that first night I decided I would never sleep again. Endless cups of black coffee and visits from the fairy Nicotine kept me going for a while, but when Fred woke up the next morning he found me curled up in the bathtub. All he did was growl, "Eat something," as though I were seeing ghosts because I was lightheaded from hunger!

And later, all the other little things. The cleaning ladies who quit after they swore they saw a woman walk into the bathroom while I was in the kitchen preparing lunch, or felt *distinctly* there was someone standing right behind them while they worked, when of course there never was. Even those stouter *putzfrauen* who after visions of their own consoled me, "It's only a little spirit cat! It means you no harm!" eventually stopped showing up when I refused to be consoled. There were countless others who quit or suffered sudden hysterical pregnancies, or simply failed to report to work after a few days of laboring in my home.

What of them? Fred will tell you one of them called him up and said, "I just can't go back there anymore – your wife just gives me the creeps." I tried to explain to him it was the lady in *white* she meant to say, the one who walked into the bathroom. White, not wife. Fred just gave me the skeptic's look of superiority and bided his time while I suffered countless tortures at the apartment's poltergeist hands.

What of the time Mimsy was over and we heard the glass shatter from all the way down the long hallway as we sat over coffee and cigarettes in the kitchen? I ran to the curio cabinet, terrified for my Wedgewood, but when I arrived there not a single thing was broken. Not a shard. And yet she heard it, too. She hasn't been back since; she doesn't even return my phone calls. Obviously she was so badly frightened by the event she cannot stand to even discuss it.

How could any of these things be explained?

How could you explain the smell? Sickly, heavy sweet perfume wafting, spiraling, enveloping, wafting where it had no business wafting, when I wore no scent around the house – in fact I rarely wore it at all, so sensitive was I to aromas of any kind – how could you explain that away?

Fred was so rarely home while I, I inhabited the house completely. I possessed the intimate knowledge of the place, with all its creaks and soft sighings; I can tell the difference between a rattling floorboard in a century-old house and something that can only be called uncanny! Was it, as Holzer and his silly wife had said, because I possessed the hooded eye and folded lid that demarcated the psychic (I thought phrenology had long gone out of style!)? After we moved in a succession of memories flooded back to me, strange precognitions I'd experienced in childhood, a flash of recognition and remembrance. It seemed I was only beginning to touch the hem of the psychic garment.

It was this place, this place, that smothered me in it.

This place where I sat, or walked around, alone for days on end. The hours listlessly spent fingering the piano while my ears strained at other sounds, the intermittent endless minutes spent fiddling with the placement of antiques on a shelf until I thought I was either mad or the house was lopsided. What did Fred know of the hours I would spend moving from room to room checking on the levelness of the picture-frames, adjusting the corners of the comforter on the bed to make sure it was straight, lighting a perfumed candle to make it smell more like a home? What did he know of the silence and the sounds?

In these quiet hours the sounds would come, slowly at first — the drip of a faucet, the faint hiss of radiator steam — then more and more, creaks and scrapings and the sound of wind when there was no wind. Some will tell you that three in the morning is the most frightening time of all; the graveyard shift is so named because most accidents happen between three and four a.m., when sailor's lore says ghosts drag their vessels down to Davy Jones. But I maintain it is three o'clock in the afternoon, when the smallest sounds are magnified, when the neighbors are away at work, their footsteps no longer comfortably perceptible through the walls and ceiling. That's when the mind takes fright at the queer sensations of being alone at home. Everywhere I looked over my shoulder in this dreadful apartment, there it was: that feeling, that sensation of being watched. And the dreadful sad uncertain scufflings in the purple curtains sent me diving into the medicine cabinet.

A growing menace seized me, possessed me, followed me at every turn through the quiet tomb of the apartment — thank god for Tessa and her padded footsteps pawing away behind me. Without her I wouldn't have the heart to go outside and glory in the strange beauty of the Church of the Ascension, or brave the shadier class of character strolling through Washington Square. Before Tessa came I spent a winter on Valium; thanks to her I doled out my prescriptions in ever-smaller portions and would have ceased the pills completely if my nerves were not so plucked by the constant pressing up of ghosts against me every day. With Valium I could maintain the cool blue and white freshness of morning and never have to acknowledge the dull and throbbing horrors of the headachy yellow afternoon.

I suppose Tessa saved my life in two ways, then.

"Don't you see," I'd tried to tell Fred so many times over the years, "The house wants me dead and it *will* have me if I do not go away." It *is* true! After five years of being haunted I have realized that it wants from me is nothing less than my very life.

Of this I have conclusive proof.

It happened one night last winter, after we'd just finished eating. I was clearing up the dishes when I found a single desiccated grape lying in the middle of my dinner plate.

"It's a portent of death!" I cried ("shrieked hysterically" Fred says). "All the life withered out of the precious grape – it's an omen from the other side! Death is all around us and it's coming for me next!"

"Sure honey," came his laconic reply. "Or maybe a mouse dropped a raisin in our kitchen."

"But we don't have mice, Fred."

We *don't have mice*!

Oh yes, the house desires my death. There is a sentient hostility in this townhouse and were it only animate I know it would reach out to from its very walls and suffocate me. Of that I am sure. That my earthly end will merely mean my reincarnation is no comfort to me now; I am only thirty-six years old. And Fred is adamant we leave. He says he can no longer stand what it is doing to me.

But I will not settle for any old modern box. I will not live just anywhere. A place with no mouldings, no archway, no built in bookshelves? No claw-footed tub? Where everything is despicably shiny and new? No, my senses cannot abide it. I need some place to show off my antiques to their best advantage, a place with a soul, where my creativity can flow. Fred will just have to pitch in and lend a hand with the house hunting; he will simply have to help me, and look harder. Or wait until I find a place I can truly love.

I look at him now and he sees the determination in my face.

"You can't beat that," Fred says finally, resignedly, slowly exhaling as the redness drains from his cheeks. "After everything that's happened, she's holding out for a fireplace."

THE NORTHERN DISPENSARY

"Built in 1831, the Northern Dispensary provided low-cost medical care, primarily to the neighborhood's poor." Bailey Parker waved her arms at the wedge-shaped three-story building as the tour group stared at her, dead-eyed. Everybody hated this part of the tour.

She tried to kindle their interest with a little celebrity name-dropping. "In 1837, a struggling young writer was treated here for a head cold. Can anyone guess who that man was?" Silence. *Come on people, I've said his name a dozen times today.* Bailey stared up at the Dispensary's red bricks; they were mellowed pinkish by age, patterned in the old style of one short end to one long. Short, long, short, long, like a signal in Morse code.

"Poe." She delivered the single syllable with a bit more jaw-clenching terseness than she intended. "Edgar Allan."

A chorus of half-hearted *ohhhs*. Perhaps Poe wasn't celebrity enough for this crowd.

"Later the Dispensary became a dental clinic and in 1986 it was sued for refusing to treat an HIV-positive patient. It's been closed and vacant ever since." She gestured to the dusty windows, empty as gaping teeth. Someone coughed in the crowd.

* * *

"How'd you do?" Her roommate Julia asked when she got home.

"Twelve dollars."

"Ouch."

Bailey sighed. She was hot, sweaty, hoarse and exhausted, and in no mood to think about the fact that she was still working tourists for tips after a decade in New York. It was a step above Starbucks in the day-job hierarchy, but only the merest step.

She let herself into the bathroom and turned on the faucet to drown out Julia's clucks of sympathy, splashing water on her crimson skin until it calmed down a bit. Still, the harsh yellow lights of the bathroom screamed a litany of flaws: fine lines, blackheads, burst blood vessels, thinning hairline. "Women over thirty should only look into the mirror under natural light," she thought as she observed the grotesque shadows the fluorescent bulbs cast under her eyes.

"Hey," Julia called from the living room. "Your phone is ringing."

Bailey snapped to attention and ran to answer it. Ten years of repeated rejection couldn't prevent her from answering every late-night phone call with a flutter of hope in her heart, a Pavlovian solicitude that impelled her to smile so that the caller on the other end could *hear* it in her voice.

"Hel-*lo*, Markus!"

A deep sigh from her agent preceded his response, as it always did. Markus was terribly world-weary, perpetually exhausted from peddling promises that mostly just ended up with him shunting his clients into background jobs on *Law & Order*. "Hi Bailey. I have a four-thirty for you tomorrow. HBO."

Eagerly, Bailey took down all the details, checked them twice, and headed straight to bed with a Mario Badescu firming masque. An audition for a high-end cable series didn't come along every day.

* * *

"Sit right there, please."

Bailey complied. A casting agent and two producers sat across from her behind a brown wooden table. The late afternoon light poured into the Tribeca loft as its ten-foot windows caught the fading sun from beyond the Hudson River.

"So," one of them began, interlacing his fingers and resting his chin on his hands while he stared at her. "How long have you been acting?"

"About five years or so," she replied, shaving a good half-decade off her resume.

"And before that?"

"I started acting right out of college." Another white lie. But there were three years of false starts, shady agents and expensive headshots that never again needed to see the light of day.

"So you've done a lot of television."

She nodded and smiled, an "I'm really listening to everything you say" smile.

He stared down at her headshot again. "Bailey Parker. That's a good name. Has a nice ring to it."

The other producer leaned forward in hushed conference.

Bailey could hear them say, "She's about the right..." and then she thought she heard him say either "age" or "face."

The casting agent smiled at Bailey. "The show's set in the 1930s," she said, by way of conversation.

"Oh that's great – I love history, anything old-fashioned." This actually was true. Bailey loved vintage clothing and the musty smell of used books. She smiled at the thought of costumes she'd get to wear if – no, *when* – she got a part on this show.

"Let me tell you a bit more about the series, Miss Parker," the first producer said, re-joining the conversation. "It's all about Jimmy Walker, New York City's so-called Diamond Mayor. He was this rich guy, a playboy –"

"Songwriter, too," interjected the other producer.

"Right. And a gambler and rum-runner. Built a casino in Central Park, and put up his mistress in a swank house in the Village that she turned into a speakeasy."

"We were looking for someone to play one of the showgirls, but looking at you..."

"We'd like you to read for the role of Betty Compton, the mayor's mistress."

Bailey's head swam. Called in for a bit part, and now this! Surely this had to mean something. Their first names started with the same letter. They even had the same number of syllables. Before they even handed her the script she knew it. She *was* Betty Compton.

Bailey breezed through the audition, fluttering her lashes and laughing breathlessly, the very embodiment of a flirtatious, free-spirited flapper.

The producers glanced at each other and conferred briefly with the casting agent, who flipped her script closed and raised an eyebrow approvingly. "That was awesome, Bailey. We'll be in touch."

"I did it," she thought as she floated out of the studio. "I have this." She'd never felt so utterly confident after an audition, not ever. All of it was finally paying off. She was dizzy with happiness. It was finally, finally happening.

* * *

Bailey got the callback the next day, as she was on her way to give a tour. She was in such a good mood she did all sorts of things she wouldn't normally do. She stopped to give change to buskers and homeless people and smiled at everyone on the street. She paused at a book-stall and bought a history of

Greenwich Village. "I might as well learn a little before I start the show," she reasoned. "Besides, it'll help with my tours." She conducted that evening's tour light-heartedly, peppering her speeches with tidbits gleaned from her new book, which she'd read tranquilly in a coffee shop before the tour began. She read it afterward, too, basking in her fifty-dollar's worth of tips and newfound feeling of contentment as the subway rattled under the East River toward Brooklyn. She felt a serene expression smoothing the worry lines away from her forehead. "I will be open to learning and new experiences," she chanted to herself. "I will be open to the universe."

And she read her new book in bed after she finished raving to Julia all about the day's resounding successes. She found her eye lingering over passages about the Northern Dispensary, the building that had so far failed to rouse much enthusiasm with any of her tour groups. She did like it so – it was such an oddly-shaped little building, and so strange and abandoned – and yet she never could seem to interest anyone else in it. The book, which to her delight she discovered dated from the 1930s, contained illustrations of the Dispensary's interior, at that time filled with dental offices and antiquated-looking equipment. Maybe she could use the book as a prop, or even better... all kinds of great ideas played in her head.

She wondered if she could say that Betty Compton had

gone there for dental work. She'd done some research on the character and discovered they were born in the same month, that Betty in 1931 would have been nearly the same age as Bailey was now. Maybe just a little younger. But not much. And, in another synergistic coincidence, the house that Jimmy Walker had bought her was right around the corner from the Northern Dispensary – at 12 Gay Street.

Bailey imagined herself telling her tour groups all about Betty and then adding with a flourish, "And I'm going to be playing her on the new HBO series *Empire City*," at which everyone would applaud and she'd offer to sign autographs that would undoubtedly become very valuable. And then one day in some not-so-distant heaven, she wouldn't have to lead tour groups at all. She wouldn't have to go to any dreadful day-job, ever again but would support herself entirely through her craft – a dream so wild she had never really honestly thought it would come true... until now.

She imagined paying off all five of her terrifyingly over-burdened credit cards, getting facials and pedicures on a regular basis, having her hair done somewhere nice instead of at student-training night at the Aveda Institute, and exuding the serene well-groomed beauty of a woman with money. Finally breathing the deep sigh of relief that poverty had for years constricted in her lungs and chest.

"It's my time at last," she thought. She fell asleep hearing applause.

* * *

A polite smattering met the end of her scene. Two days later, Bailey was at her callback.

She looked up to see the two producers she'd met at her earlier audition conferring with the showrunner. Why didn't they seem as enthusiastic as before? Bailey felt the cold sweat of dread. This couldn't be happening. She'd nailed it.

"Bailey," the showrunner called. "Can you come here a minute?"

She walked over to them, smiling brightly. "Yes?"

The showrunner nodded. "That's it. The face."

Said smile quickly faded.

"What's wrong?" Bailey asked.

"Looking at you now… well, there's something about your face that's a little anachronistic for the period. We're looking for that heart-shaped, Gibson girl-type face, you know?"

"Maybe we can get you some background work," the casting agent offered helpfully.

As Bailey walked out of the office she thought she heard someone say, "…a little on the old side for a showgirl."

* * *

Click. The bathroom light switched on and the yellow bulbs buzzed.

Her face. Something was wrong with her face.

They hadn't said anything at her first audition, only her callback. What was different about her callback? She couldn't think of anything.

She scrutinized herself from all angles. How could she be too old for Betty Compton? They were the same age… a little old for a showgirl maybe ("Asshole," she thought) but that couldn't be it, that couldn't be the problem… She frowned at herself, then smiled.

Wait a minute. That was it.

She smiled again. Her smile… she'd been smiling in the second scene she read. Grinning broadly, flashing her million dollar smile, giving them the old pearly whites… of course. People in the '30s didn't have pearly whites. They had little, gritty, itty, bitty grey teeth.

She gasped in horror at the realization.

Bailey stared at the offending orthodonture. Those babies were capped, bleached and Insivaligned. Just blindingly, dazzlingly white enough to get her barred from any period roles. These massive, fabricated, modern teeth, these alien teeth that were not a real part of her. Bailey stood there staring for, well, she didn't quite know how long.

Her roommate knocked on the bathroom door. "Time to come out, B."

"Thanks," Bailey said, unlocking the latch. Julia was a good soul to put up with a roommate whose monomania resulted in exorbitant hours spent in the shared bathroom.

"This came for you," Julia said, handing her a little brown box.

"Thanks again."

"What is it?"

"Just something I bought off Ebay."

She took the thing hurriedly into her room and stuffed it under the bed unopened, alongside the others. Julia stared at the closed door with her customary sympathy.

Even after Bailey's Ambien kicked in, her sleep was shallow and restless. She woke up with the blinding headache that signaled she'd been grinding and clenching her teeth all through the wee hours. She always did that when she was stressed, displacing her worries into her much-abused jaw. One of these worries? How an actress with no health insurance was going to pay for the $500 mouth-guard her dentist recommended to protect her costly cosmetic dental work.

She took two Advil and swam groggily through her tour that day. It went badly, to say the least, the crowd picking up on her bitter aura. She lingered longer than usual on the many West Village habitations of Edgar Allan Poe, expounding on his crushing poverty, ill luck, and career of heartbreaking disappointment. She felt a vicious sense of refreshment, like purging, as she described the wretchedness of the various bohemians who had lived and struggled and been utterly destroyed by their artistic lives. "Dylan Thomas, he drank himself to death, Dorothy Parker did, too." The group, a gaggle of chubby middle-school teachers from Des Moines, seemed depressed when it was over.

Bailey did not mention Betty Compton. She never wanted to think about Betty Compton again. Really, there was very little of interest in that story anyway.

The day was a typically dreary November stew of wind and clouds and early darkness, and by five o'clock, as she squeezed onto a rush-hour laden train, oppressive twilight had already engulfed the city. Bailey steadied her hand on the silver pole in the center of the dank subway car, one hand among many. There were dozens of people in this car alone, hundreds on the train, thousands of them underground in this fair city at this precise moment – how could she ever have thought herself special, different? Tears sprang unbidden to her eyes and she gazed up at the ceiling to stop them spilling over. As filled with hope and certainty as she'd been before, she was now completely adrift on a sea of self-loathing and recrimination.

"You've chased this stupid, pointless dream for so long now you've backed yourself into a corner," she scolded herself. "You're thirty years old. Talentless. Poor. No prospects. No hope. Too modern looking for a period role. Too long in the tooth to play a showgirl." Long in the tooth! She laughed out loud at her choice of words. People stared at her but she didn't care. She laughed and laughed, imagining how her massive teeth must look to them as she threw her head back in the great big heaving horse laugh of complete and utter despair.

It's amazing what a wide berth people will give a person who is laughing to herself. Before long Bailey found she had a seat with plenty of room around it. She calmed down and wiped a few rogue tears from her cheeks, pulled her book out of her bag and began to read. Her eyes lingered on an interesting footnote containing a host of macabre factoids about 19th century dentistry.

For instance, not everyone would need to avail themselves of the services of a clinic. Apparently, one could get a mail-order diploma and practice in one's house, which opened up the profession to anybody with a kitchen table. Ergo dentistry was not considered the noble, lucrative profession it is today and, naturally, suspicions of quackery plagued tooth-pullers. Another fact: dentists had ample supplies of opium and morphine. Though so did everyone else, morphine being obtainable over the counter in any pharmacy until 1914. However, it was with dentists that the criminal classes were most associated, as another common type of quackery involved patients malingering for the purposes of obtaining opiates.

Another curious side-note: Ninety percent of standard modern dental equipment remains virtually identical to that of the 1800s; for example, the old manual drill with interchangeable burs is different from that which accosts you on your average dental visit only by virtue of not having a motor. Otherwise, it is almost exactly the same. And that chair and rinse-and-spit setup? According to the book, one could find a nearly identical configuration in 1837. Pre-electricity, lights were coal-operated, or sometimes illuminated by manual foot pedals, as were drills, but that's about the only difference. Anesthetic syringes today are carbon copies of their predecessors. And the extraction forceps? The same. Only nowadays there tend to be fewer extractions.

Bailey was so completely absorbed in her book that she failed to notice the people around her were staring at her. But then she heard a sound, an odd, grating sound. She looked up, listening. Crunnnnch.... It was –

Bailey's teeth were gnashing together of their own accord, loudly, disgustingly. She exerted on them a pressure so intense it seemed she aimed to grind her tooth enamel into dust, bite through her lips, sever her own jawbone. An electric jolt shot through her temple with the lightning-flash of pain.

Horrified, she bolted from her seat and pushed her way to the subway doors. She darted through them as soon as the train reached the next stop and she ran through a maze of warehouses in the gloaming of industrial Brooklyn, and all the way home.

* * *

They were mocking her.

She looked in the mirror. They *were* mocking her. They were abominable, hideous, disfiguring; they were gleaming white reminders of her failure, mocking her. Look at what your vanity has wrought!

They threw the aging decrepitude of the rest of her face into relief, a face which, just then, was curdled with anxiety and stained and puffy with tears. Upon arriving home she received a phone call from the manager at the tour company. She was fired. The customers said she frightened them.

Fired! With no notice, no goodbye, no one-last-tour so she could scrape together any possible emergency funds she might need, oh no. Unceremoniously, suddenly, and without warning, dropped. Let go. Finished. Over. The fate of the washed-up actress.

She laughed bitterly, and her teeth laughed right back at her.

They were punishing her. As she smiled they bared themselves, turning her smile into a gaping, grimacing, skeletal rictus. She hated them.

She couldn't stand them any more.

Reaching under the sink, she pulled out the five or six boxes that contained what she needed and set to work. She laid the objects before her on the counter-top, the objects she'd thought to use as props on her tours. They were old, but like the book said, the technology is virtually unchanged. They'd do the trick.

She must have made more noise than she'd anticipated, because presently there came a rather frantic-sounding knock at the door.

"Bailey, Bailey, are you OK!?" Julia sounded upset. "What's going on?"

"Nothing," Bailey replied.

"Can I come in?"

"Of course." She opened the door.

Julia clapped her hands over her mouth when she saw her. "Oh my god," came muffled from within.

Scattered on the counter atop spilled tissue paper were the no-longer-gleaming dental instruments, worn with age, and a single ivory inlaid box, that contained in all their rattling, bloody glory, every single one of Bailey's white, gleaming, perfectly modern teeth. Yes, all thirty-two of them.

"I got them all," she said.

BOROUGHS OF THE DEAD

A Note on the Text

Every effort has been made to proofread this book to professional standards. If you find an error in *Boroughs of the Dead*, please email boroughsofthedead@gmail.com.

ABOUT THE AUTHOR

Andrea Janes lives in Brooklyn with her husband, across the street from a cemetery and a high-voltage ConEd substation. She hopes that one day, maybe during a thunderstorm, this combination will result in some really cool zombie action. This is her first book.

10121099R00083

Made in the USA
Charleston, SC
09 November 2011